Karmel [Ja...] st publish... book was a col... st *Zauri* [*Fifteen Wounds*], pul... ...e has published other short stories, novels, and poetry. Her short stories have appeared in a number of anthologies, incl...ing *Best European Fiction 2017*, and have been adapted fo... the theatre (*Ecografías* [*Ultrasound*], 2010). *Her Mother's ...ds* (published originally in Basque in 2006 as *Amaren ...k*) was her first novel, and was well received by readers ...critics alike. This novel was a bestseller and won a ...ber of awards, including the Igartza Prize and the Euskadi ...lata award. It has also been adapted for film, and was ...sented at the 2013 San Sebastian International Film ...ival.

Kristin Addis has worked for nearly thirty years as a translator. She translates primarily between Spanish or Basque and English, and is one of few who translate directly from Basque into English. She specialises in literary translation, which she especially enjoys, and has translated short stories, novels, and poetry. She has also translated various works about the Basque language and culture. Kristin has spent many years in the Basque Country; she currently resides in Iowa with her family.

Her Mother's Hands

Translated from Basque
by Kristin Addis

Karmele Jaio

PARTHIAN

This book has been selected to receive financial assistance from English PEN's PEN Translates programme, supported by Arts Council England. English PEN exists to promote literature and our understanding of it, to uphold writers' freedoms around the world, to campaign against the persecution and imprisonment of writers for stating their views, and to promote the friendly co-operation of writers and the free exchange of ideas. www.englishpen.org

Parthian, Cardigan SA43 1ED
www.parthianbooks.com
Her Mother's Hands first published as *Amaren eskuak* in 2006.
First published in 2018.
© Karmele Jaio 2018
© This translation by Kristin Addis 2018
ISBN 978-1-912109-55-5
Editor: Susie Wild
Cover design by RJPHA
Typeset by Elaine Sharples
Printed in EU by Pulsio SARL
Published with the financial support of the Welsh Books Council, English PEN and the Etxepare Basque Institute.
British Library Cataloguing in Publication Data
A cataloguing record for this book is available from the British Library.

CYNGOR LLYFRAU CYMRU
WELSH BOOKS COUNCIL

For Karmele Eiguren and Joseba Jaio

The little girl is on the beach, at the water's edge. She has built a wall of wet sand and given it the shape of the prow of a boat. She sits inside, gazing at the white waves. Her legs are stretched out in front of her. Her feet are wrinkled, as are her hands. The water advances. A wave attacks the prow from the left but the girl repairs it immediately and remains on her knees, one strap of her bathing suit falling from her shoulder, ready to respond quickly to the next attack. She knows that the sea will win the battle in the end and that the waves will wash away her ship of sand like a tongue licks away ice cream, but even so, she defends her small realm with tooth and claw. With her jaw firmly set.

When Nerea sees herself in the photograph from the beach, it brings back the smell of the summers she spent at the seaside as a child. She smells the cream her mother used to put on her, feels the slide of her mother's hand putting it on her back. She remembers her father lying under the beach umbrella or walking along the water's edge, while her mother lay in the hammock. Like today. Her mother is lying down today as well, right in front of her, but in a hospital bed, not a hammock. The old photo she brought to show her mother is in her purse, and she sits without moving in the white hospital chair, looking at her mother's hands.

Her mother's hands rest on top of the sheet. Without moving. As if made of stone. As if the blood in her veins had turned to stagnant water. Her hands cover the name of the hospital, as if she wanted to hide where she is. As if even in her sleep, she were trying not to worry anyone. Just as through the years she hid so many sighs and tears, drying them on her kitchen apron, Nerea's mother is now trying to hide with her hands the word *hospital* printed on the cloth. But through her fingers she has left part of the word visible. *Tal*. And Nerea smiles to read it, because *tale* means 'story' in the language of her husband, and because it occurs to her that ever since her mother was admitted, she has been living in a sort of story. The smile freezes on Nerea's lips then, as she gazes at her mother's hands.

Her mother seems to have been living in a story ever since she was admitted. In her eyes one can see little girls playing on the school playground, and hear their shrieks and laughter. When she opens her eyes, she smiles at Xabier and Nerea, but she does not recognise her children. Nevertheless, she smiles at them, and this lightens the load of their sadness a little. Just a little.

Her mother has spent more than a week now between these blue and white sheets, and Nerea thinks if things don't change much, they may well still be here at Christmas. She and her mother are now alone in the room. Her mother is asleep. She sleeps almost the whole day, like little children do. The bed by the window is empty and only coughs from nearby rooms break the silence. Nerea hears her own breath and her mother's, in and out, and the sound of their breathing makes it impossible for her to concentrate on reading the magazines she brought, or look calmly at the pictures either. So she sits still, gazing at her mother's hands. The veins in her hands look like highways full of curves.

These are hands that have sheltered, the way the nest in the branches shelters the bird. Her mother's hand cupping her chin. This is how Nerea pictures her mother's protection. Her mother's hand on her chin in a black and white photograph.

She looks at the empty bed before her and imagines a little girl jumping on it with her younger brother. They are throwing pillows at each other and laughing. Children's laughter. They fill the room with laughter. She hears her mother's voice in the distance, asking them not to make noise. The downstairs neighbours will come up. But they keep jumping and laughing, like on the school playground.

Suddenly she sees herself laughing. Jumping on the bed. Her little brother has disappeared from her side. As has her mother's voice from afar. All of a sudden she leaps upwards and, as if wings had sprung from her shoulders, she ends up high above the ground, hanging in the air. And she sees herself, as if pushed by the wind, flying out the hospital window.

Like a gull that crosses the ocean seeking fish, she flies over the city as if seeking something. After passing over red rooftops and smoky chimneys, she enters the living room of an old house through a half-open window. An old Telefunken television stands in the middle of the room with a framed photograph on top of it. There they are. There she finds her mother's hands. They are black and white hands and they rest on a young girl's chin. And suddenly everything goes black and white around her, and she hears a voice from afar, saying 'Nerea, raise your head,' asking her to look at the photographer, please, and the

3

smell of those hands enters her nostrils, the smell of bleach and Marseille soap. And she hears a tune. It comes from the kitchen radio. Her mother is listening to the radio in the kitchen and darning her brother's soccer socks for the millionth time, her glasses on the end of her nose. Nerea closes her eyes and opens them, and again sees her mother's hand, but now it holds a pencil sharpened with a knife and she is writing the household accounts in an old notebook, *tomatoes five pesetas*, *eggs seven pesetas*, and she underlines the total hard, almost breaking the point of the pencil. Now she sees her mother in a bedroom, sitting on the edge of a small bed. She strokes the forehead of the little girl in the bed, while singing her a song. She won't stop until the little girl falls asleep.

As soon as she hears the singing, Nerea looks at her mother there between the blue and white hospital sheets. But her mother's lips are not moving. She lies absolutely still in the hospital bed. Nevertheless, Nerea still hears the song from far away. It won't stop until the little girl falls asleep. And just for a moment, she feels the hands before her caress her forehead. Even though they look like stone.

A telephone call turned her world upside down eight days ago. It might have been nine; she has lost track of time since then, but the moment is etched on her mind. She was walking down the street and the voice on the other end of the telephone hit her in the stomach like a shot. Her legs suddenly stopped walking and she simply stood in the middle of the street without moving, as if a tree had fallen in her path. Just like she used to stop in the middle of the hallway when her mother tried to take her to the doctor as a child, moving neither forward nor back. Feet turned to stone. It is her brother's voice. They found their mother on the street. Lost. 'They found her lost like a child,' says her brother on the other end of the phone. His voice is calm and neutral. He sounds as if he's reading a report at the office. As if he were afraid that allowing any drama in his voice would suddenly open a reservoir of emotions. He would prefer to have them all seep out through the cracks. Slowly. She calls Lewis and asks him to pick up their daughter from school. She can't, she'll explain later, her mother is in the hospital. *In hospital*.

She arrived at the hospital eight days ago, telephone still in hand. She asked the nurse anxiously if Luisa Izagirre had been admitted, and the nurse had told her that they had taken her from the emergency room straight to Neurology. It sounded like a heavy word. Neurology. At least half a kilo. A pound, as her mother and Aunt Dolores would say. And she truly feels the weight of a one-pound stone on her neck, because even though she hadn't wanted to accept it, she had been worried that something was happening to her mother. This makes her feel guilty. The first time she saw herself in the bathroom mirror at the hospital, she understood that she was guilty, because she had not accepted – until her mother was admitted to the hospital – that a red flag had gone up, and she had been wondering if something was happening to her mother. But she had done nothing. Like a child, she had stuck her fingers in her ears in order not to hear. The signs were right before her eyes and she hadn't wanted to see them.

How many times this week has she remembered the day when her mother was making croquettes and lost her train of thought? She had gone into the kitchen in her mother's house and found her staring at a ball of dough in her hands as if frozen, with no idea whether to put it in the flour, the egg, or the breadcrumbs. As if her mind had gone completely blank for a moment. 'Mum, in the flour,' she murmured, and she still doesn't know how she ever dared to tell her mother how to make croquettes. Tell an Izagirre. The youngest daughter of the Izagirre Restaurant family. Her mother looked right at her, with the dough still in her hand, and it seemed to Nerea she might have stayed like that forever if the pan hadn't begun to smoke. She still can't forget the lost look in her mother's eyes. It's etched on her mind. When her mother grasped the situation, she smiled to hide her fear, and Nerea smiled back so her mother wouldn't see the worry on her face. The red flag had been up since then but, like a child, she had covered her eyes with her hands so she wouldn't see it waving. And now she drags the weight of the word *neurology* like a punishment, from the hospital to the office, from the office home, from home back to the hospital, leaving behind a dark trail of guilt. A trail darker than the dark blue worn by fishermen.

Sitting in the white chair at the hospital, she spends the day looking at her mother's hands as if she believed those hands would speak to her. As if, in those hands, she would find the answers to the thousands of questions she had never asked her mother. As if she would be able to hear the words and thoughts her mother had hidden for so many years. Simply by looking at her hands, the hands that now cover the first two syllables of the word *hospital*. She can read *tal* between her mother's fingers. *Tale*, a story in Nerea's husband's language. Nerea smiles because it seems that her mother has lived in a story since she was admitted, but her smile freezes as she looks at the bed by the window. The sheets are rumpled, as if someone has been jumping on the bed.

2

She wakes with a headache. Her brains are tied in a knot. She was dreaming all night. As she sits on the side of the bed and begins to put on her slippers, she tries to remember what she dreamed, but nothing comes to her. She imagines a giant question mark over her head like the ones in the cartoons Maialen watches. Lewis is still half asleep in the bed. He mumbles something but she doesn't understand. Not because he said it in English, but because he barely moved his lips. She looks at her husband, waiting for him to speak again, but Lewis says nothing more and goes back to sleep after moving into the now-empty, warm side of the bed. The English must have imperialism in their blood, she thinks. Lewis always takes over her side of the bed as soon as she leaves it empty. Sometimes she thinks he is hoping she'll get up just so he can have it.

She puts the coffee on and goes to her daughter's room. Maialen is still asleep. A book has fallen to the floor under her bed. It is *Alice in Wonderland*, which Lewis reads to her at night. A page folded over when the book fell. Nerea picks up the book and smooths the page with her hand. The page is illustrated. Alice is looking at a cat sitting in a tree and she asks it a question. Nerea begins to read:

'Would you tell me, please, which way I ought to go from here?'

'That depends a good deal on where you want to get to,' said the Cat.

'I don't much care where—' said Alice.

'Then it doesn't matter which way you go.'

Nerea raises her head from the book. The conversation has made her remember a nightmare from the night before. She also was asking someone something in her dreams and waited for an answer looking up, like Alice. But she can't remember whom she was asking. Or what she was asking either. Sitting on her knees, she looks at the cat's wide smile. Until she remembers the coffee. Then she puts the book on the night table and goes to the kitchen. The smell of coffee fills the whole house.

While she drinks her coffee, she can't get the image of the cat out of her mind. And its smile. If one doesn't know where one wants to get to, it doesn't matter which way one goes. That's what the cat said. That's stupid, she thinks. It's stupid to sit here thinking about what a cat in a story said, with all she has to do today. It's Lewis' fault. Almost every night he reads a chapter to Maialen while they wait for her to get home from work. She should ask him to read some other story to their daughter, she thinks, before Alice drives them all mad, but she knows what he will say. He grew up with this story, his mother used to tell it to him when he was little, in Oxford, and he wants his daughter to know it as well as he does. Besides, when she's away from home, she can hardly control what bedtime stories Lewis tells their daughter.

Yesterday she was late getting home. Late home from the office, as usual. Maialen was asleep by then, as she often is. After spending the morning at the hospital, Nerea had spent the entire afternoon in the editorial office at the newspaper since she was on the late shift. Lewis opened the door as she was about to put her key in the lock. Seeing her husband saying good evening by the door made her think of an English butler, he stands so tall and straight, he is so polite, so attentive. The years he has spent away from his country have done nothing to nullify Lewis' English soul. Even now, when he walks past her, she sometimes thinks she can smell tea and biscuits.

She goes to Maialen's room and peeks in at her sleeping quietly. It makes her think of the way her mother was sleeping in the hospital.

When she gets home late from work, she always asks Lewis about their day. And when Lewis starts to tell her all about it, she wonders how they would manage if he weren't home all day working on his translations. What would happen if he worked outside the home too and came home late, as she does when she has to work the late shift at the newspaper? She shivers. That's why she doesn't want to think about it too much. She envies Lewis, working at home, playing with Maialen all afternoon, reading her stories at night. But Lewis has often told her he'd rather work outside the home, getting out of the house is often a relief. He says it in English. *A relief*. And he repeats it in Spanish, with the English accent he will never lose. There is only one word he says without an English accent: Maialen. He has no translation for it in his mind.

They always speak English to each other because they spoke English when they met, the year Nerea was studying at Oxford, but Lewis knows more and more Spanish and even a little Basque. This year he started studying at a Basque language school, almost under duress. Nerea convinced her husband with the argument that he would need it to understand the homework his daughter would bring home from school, but it wasn't easy to convince him. She doesn't know if her husband will ever understand how important the language is to her. She doesn't know if he will ever understand the effort so many people have made and still make to keep the language alive. How could he understand, she often thinks, when English is spoken all over the world? How will he ever understand that her language is as fragile as a newborn, that it needs protection as much as their daughter does?

Nerea often laughs at him for the English accent he can't get rid of. Maybe because she remembers how, when they first met in England, Lewis had laughed at her accent and her friend Maite's. Lewis used to say that in addition to drinking beer like men, they both sounded very funny when they spoke English. And then he laughed. Lewis laughed with beer foam on his lips. When Lewis first met these foreign women in the pub, he was astonished at the way they drank. He later confessed it was the first time he had seen such a thing: after drinking so much beer, instead of starting to dance or shout, they stayed on their stools by the bar, one hand on the pitcher of beer and the other holding a cigarette, getting up only to go to the bathroom. Like men. Like English men. *Like English men.*

Maite had tried to explain to Lewis that Basque girls were more practiced at such things than the local girls, that they often went to *txosnas*, refreshment stands at festivals, as if Lewis knew what *txosnas* were. Nerea had met Lewis in Oxford through Maite. Maite was her best friend there, her fellow student, flatmate and greatest support. Nerea often thinks that without Maite's support, she would barely have made it through the year she spent abroad. The year she spent in Oxford was not an easy one for her.

She had arrived there hurt and empty. After the boyfriend she had dated for four years at home had disappeared, she had made the decision to go to Oxford to study. Karlos had disappeared into thin air. One day he was there, and the next he had disappeared from the country and from ordinary life. She had gone to Oxford hoping to erase the memories that left a sour taste in her mouth. But the wounds she tried to cover with beer foam in the pubs there ran deeper than she had thought. The kind that open again just when you think they've scarred over.

They had started going out when Nerea was seventeen, and when she was a week short of turning twenty-two, Karlos disappeared. He gave her no explanation. Like the other two young men from the same town who disappeared with him, he gave no one any explanation. The political situation of the time sucked Karlos in like a drain sucks in water and carried him off to some hidden underground place. Like Alice falling down the rabbit hole, he fell and has lived in a different world ever since. Nerea has tried a million times to imagine what that world must be like. No one around her asked about Karlos after he disappeared, except his dog Blackie and the police. The police came to her house and asked her a million questions, trying to figure out where Karlos had gone. But they never found him. She did, though. Nerea found him every night in her worst nightmares.

The questions surrounding Karlos' disappearance played in her mind on an endless loop and she often wondered, if she hadn't taken the opportunity to go study at Oxford, whether she would have gone on forever like that, waiting for Karlos, a member of the local widows' club. She had fled, but her nightmares had followed her. Karlos appeared in her dreams, smoke or fire all around him, carrying a weapon. She saw him sweating, hiding, fleeing, running wounded in the mountains. Other times she would see him walking on a crowded street in a big city, wearing dark glasses so the police wouldn't recognise him. She sometimes even dreamed he appeared at the door of her apartment in Oxford, begging her to please let him sleep there, he had nowhere to sleep, please. Saying 'just one night and you'll never see me again.' Nerea would wake up in a sweat. 'It's okay, it's okay,' her flatmate Maite would say then, smoothing her clammy forehead without knowing what else to say.

Maite would never have guessed it then, but it was thanks to one of her joyful shrieks that Nerea would find her husband in Oxford. It happened one time when they had been drinking heavily. Maite let out a shriek, leaning onto the bar of a dark and smoky pub, and the half-closed eyes of all the patrons suddenly snapped open, as if a loud and exotic bird had entered that dark place, shaking its feathers with abandon. The tall blond boy had come over to them then, interested in learning the reason for that shriek of laughter. Everything they told him then about the Basques had seemed exotic to Lewis. And even now he has not yet become entirely accustomed to the way of life in Nerea's country. 'It's because he's so very English, poor fellow,' Nerea often says in despair.

If Lewis hadn't approached the two foreign girls in that pub, Nerea wouldn't have found him at home last night when she came back from work, in the kitchen, offering her a reheated dinner. While she ate, she told him about her day: after spending the morning at the hospital, she had a quick snack at a bar and then raced to the editorial office, where she stayed until press time. While she was telling him this, she could feel her heartbeat in her temples. Every time she started talking, she felt a sharp stab. It happened when she smoked too much. She had arrived home from the office yesterday with her head full of smoke. After dinner, she put her fingers on her temples, closed her eyes and heaved a sigh. Lewis didn't take his eyes off her. He stared at her like a prison inmate looking at a visitor. Thirsting for news from life outside.

She told Lewis she had to call her aunt, Dolores, the one who lives in Frankfurt. She and Xabier had agreed to call her. They hadn't called earlier because they didn't want to worry her, and they knew that as soon as she found out her sister was in the hospital, she would be on the first plane to Bilbao. Nerea was going to call her the next morning.

Nerea wants to see her aunt. The last time she saw her was in the summer. She used to visit only at Christmas, but since Nerea and Xabier's father died, she visits more often, with their uncle Sebastian. Nerea's mother's face used to light up when her sister visited. They would tell each other stories about growing up in their village, stories about when they worked in the family restaurant mostly. Often-told stories about the Izagirre Restaurant. As soon as they were married, they both left the small town on the coast where they were born for unfamiliar cities, but when they saw each other they always reminisced about the years they spent in their village. Seeing how much they enjoy telling stories from the old days, Nerea has thought more than once that their childhood years in the village must have been the happiest of their lives. Since she knows how much her mother appreciated Aunt Dolores' visits, Nerea is sure that seeing her sister will help her find her way out of this dream she has fallen into.

This morning, she eats breakfast and immediately starts dialing the country code for Germany. Aunt Dolores is shocked to hear that Nerea's mother has been admitted to the hospital, and says she will be there as soon as she can. She'll look at flights and call right back, and why on earth hadn't Nerea called sooner. Nerea tries to calm her down, but she knows well enough that calming her Aunt Dolores is an exercise in futility. *Impossible job*, as Lewis would say.

3

Nerea can't get used to the smell of medicine and hospital food. When it enters her nostrils, the world suddenly becomes fragile and she tries not to tread too heavily on the white hospital floors. She walks the corridors almost on tiptoe, as if the ground beneath her feet might fall away at any moment. She steps on the hospital floor as if it were made of cellophane. As if it were as fragile as the cellophane on bouquets for new mothers.

As fragile as Maialen when she was a newborn. Nerea had noticed the same smell of medicine and hospital food when they brought her here in an ambulance in her seventh month of pregnancy. Maialen was in a hurry to meet the world. With her hand on her belly at seven months, Nerea had told her too much about the world and Maialen was born wanting to see it all, almost two months early. Hurry. It was no surprise that she was in such a hurry since for seven months she had felt her mother hurrying to and fro while her belly grew. In the office they kept asking Nerea when she was going to take her maternity leave. 'Not yet, I still feel fine,' she would say.

Seven months and seven hours. It was a seven-hour labour. But Nerea doesn't remember much about it. Pain, she remembers pain. And that she was gritting her teeth. And that she was sweating. And that they kept saying 'easy, easy does it.' But not much else. She barely remembers that Lewis was there. Seeing Maialen erased everything that came before from her memory. When she saw a part of her body that had suddenly become another body, she had started to cry. But not because of the pain. A part of her, her most fragile part, had left her body, stained with her blood and, as if she saw herself stained with her blood, the tears flowed from her eyes, tears she could not stop.

She goes down the hall and stops in front of her mother's room. As she goes in she thinks she must be mistaken, for there, in addition to her mother, are two women, one lying on the bed next to her mother's and the other standing beside the first. Nerea's brother, who should have spent the night with their mother, is not there. Until the day before, her mother had had the room to herself. That's why Nerea is surprised to see that the other bed is now taken.

The two women greet her at the same time, as if they were a single person. The one who is standing looks like the daughter of the patient. She has exactly the same face, only thirty years younger.

'Are you the daughter?' the younger one asks her right away in Spanish, and Nerea notices a Galician accent in those first words. She nods yes. She doesn't want to make a sound since she sees her mother is sleeping. She is asleep, like Maialen in bed this morning, and with the pretext of picking up a magazine that has fallen to the floor, Nerea goes straight over to her, with a shy smile at the two women.

From the other side of the room, the younger woman explains that Xabier went home at midnight. She sent him home. She told him to go ahead and leave and not to worry, since she had to stay anyway and there was no need for both of them to be there. And that's why her brother is not there now. Xabier had told her what had happened. It was a real pity. He had also told her that their mother lived alone since her husband died, and that really is a pity, to live alone. She lives with her mother, she explains, but now here they are, her mother is under observation... And so on.

The woman fills the room with words, and Nerea feels like she's drowning in all those words and it's so hot in there. She starts taking off her clothes quickly. Her jacket, her sweater... she thinks she could almost take off her shirt too. She looks at her mother's hair and notices the white roots. She needs to have her hair dyed. Then she looks at her mother's mouth. Her lips are parted and she looks calm. Nerea has rarely seen her mother so calm. She has always seen her with her lips tightly closed, jaw clenched. And always doing something, never still. Until now, she has seen her mother still only in photographs, and now she looks as if she's in a photo.

But all of a sudden she starts moving and, as if she sensed that Nerea was near, sighs and suddenly opens her eyes. Nerea moves closer with her hand to her chest. Her heart leaps like a rabbit. It leaps, almost jumping out of her throat. Her mother's eyes are wide open, she is just looking at Nerea, who thinks that her mother recognises her. Her mother smiles at her and she says 'Mum, Mum' two times, barely opening her lips, but her mother doesn't answer. She only smiles. Seeing that smile, Nerea remembers a photo of her mother as a young woman. It is an old photograph taken in the kitchen of the Izagirre Restaurant, and in it are all the women who worked together with her mother in the kitchen. Her mother has shown her that photo many times. Dolores is there with Nerea's mother, and their mother Petra and Aunt Bittori appear too. When she goes home she must find that photo to show it to her mother, she thinks, to wake her memories. So that by remembering the old days at the Izagirre Restaurant, she might also remember who she is now.

Her mother does not recognise her. She reaches out the hand she had at her chest to her mother, and her mother takes it and strokes it with the same tenderness with which she used to stroke Nerea's forehead every night when she was little, while she sang her that song. When she remembers the song, Nerea feels a lump in her throat. Then she realises that the women beside her are looking at her, and she feels as if she were naked in the middle of the supermarket. She would like to be able to pull a curtain across between them.

The younger woman is still talking. She says that Luisa was smiling at night too, as if she were dreaming about lovely things. And she adds that she slept only a little, watching over the two older women's sleep, and her mother's name is Pilar and so is hers, but people call her Pili, and she says lots of other things that Nerea doesn't listen to. She is used to simply shutting her ears sometimes. She learned it from her job. It is one of the few good things she has learned from journalism. Often in a press conference, when she thinks she has enough information, she closes her ears and starts to think about her own things. She does the same now with Pilar or Pili or whatever her name is.

Nerea wants her to shut up once and for all. She feels like Pili is trying to force her way into the black and white photo in her mind, pushing and shoving the women in the kitchen of the Izagirre Restaurant. She has a voice like bagpipes and the sound of bagpipes is getting mixed up in Nerea's mind with the song her mother used to sing to her at night. All she wants is for Pili to shut up and for her mother to start talking.

But her mother does not speak. She looks at Nerea for a moment, but then her gaze wanders and gets lost in the open space of the white room, and with that loss of focus, Nerea too feels that she has lost something or that something has escaped from her. Like water slips between the fingers.

Pili's chatter has not stopped. Her mother Pilar, on the other hand, hasn't opened her mouth. And unlike Nerea's mother, she offers no smiles. She just stares at the raindrops on the windowpane. Silently, as if she were not listening to her daughter Pili's shower of words either. As if her head too were in a black and white photograph.

Then, from that shower of words a sentence reaches Nerea's ears. A sentence that emerges from all those words, like gold from among the stones in a prospector's sieve. Pili says her mother talked at night. And Nerea doesn't know whose mother she is talking about, and the question leaps out of her before she can think. Who talked, was it her mother, she asks, astonished, without letting go of her mother's hand. She is unsettled, for this is no small thing: since they found her mother wandering, she has said nothing at all. She has not once opened her mouth. And Nerea has been trying to remember her voice these last few days, but she can't.

'Yes, she spoke,' says Pili. She doesn't know for sure if she was awake or asleep. As soon as Xabier left, she started talking, and she said a name over and over. But now Pili can't remember what it was. 'What was it again?' she says, looking up at the ceiling. Nerea stares at the whites of the woman's eyes. She waits as if turned to stone, looking at her. She would give good money to know what name her mother calls out in her sleep, but she doesn't ask. She keeps quiet, at a loss for words. She wants to ask but she can't say anything.

19

'What was it?' Pili repeats, this time covering her eyes with her hand. 'What could it have been?'

Nerea realises that this is the first time she has actually wanted Pili to speak. She has pricked up her ears. Her eyes are wide open.

And Pilar, who is still looking at the raindrops on the window, barely moves her lips to say a name.

'Herman,' she says, without raising her eyes from the window.

Pili's mother tosses out the name like a stone. *Herman*. The name falls on Nerea's ears like a stone onto a frozen lake.

'That's it,' says Pili, 'Herman.'

And she adds that Luisa said the name over and over and that Herman must be her husband, right? Xabier had told her that he had died ten years ago...

Nerea hears nothing more, only a voice from far away. For a moment she thinks that Pili exists only in her imagination and she must be dreaming and the damned cat from the story must surely now appear before her eyes. Laughing. Laughing at her. When she hears the man's name she feels that the hospital floor should tear as if it were made of cellophane.

She looks Pili in the face but says nothing to her. She is still at a loss for words. She doesn't tell Pili that her father's name was not Herman, but Paulo, Paulo Etxebarria, and she must have made up the name Herman or heard it wrong, her mother never knew any man named Herman. She thinks all this but says nothing, just bites her lip and then excuses herself to go to the restroom. She smokes a cigarette sitting on the toilet.

4

'Rough seas today,' the sailor said to the captain of the Urkiolamendi. The captain, eyes on the horizon, made no answer. Young Herman, on deck with them, saw a chasm in the captain's eyes, a deep dark hole and, realising that the ship was rocking more and more, suddenly thought about what he had left behind on dry land, and he saw a girl in the town square at Sunday's dance, felt his rough hands on her waist, hands now torn by the sea. The motion of the ship was becoming more turbulent. The waves pounded it from one side then the other, more and more violently, and suddenly Herman felt the water crash over him from top to bottom, as if he were in a downpour. Soaked from top to bottom. Before he had time to clear the water from his eyes, another downpour crashed over him. Saltwater on his lips, barely able to open his eyes, he heard the captain shout to tie himself to the ship with a rope, tie himself on with a rope. And as if it were an umbilical cord tying him to life, he began to tie the rope around his waist, but suddenly there was a blow stronger than the others, *bang*, and it knocked the rope out of his hands. Like a woman stealing a baby from another, the sea swept Herman from the Urkiolamendi. Herman heard nothing more. He didn't hear the captain shouting for him, or Txiki barking. The last thing he saw was a life preserver knocked this way and that by the waves and as he was trying to reach it, everything went black.

5

Airports look a lot like hospitals. There are white waiting rooms there as well, most of the people waiting are pale, as in the hospital, and the stewardesses walking behind the pilots look just like nurses walking behind doctors. Both with the same arrogant stride, thinks Nerea.

The plane from Frankfurt is delayed. A woman's voice announces it over the loudspeaker, the same voice that is on loudspeakers everywhere. Nerea used to hear the same voice in the Tesco supermarket in Oxford announcing the day's special offers, and she hears this same voice today in the hospital where her mother lies, paging the doctors. While she waits, she tries to remember Aunt Dolores' face and sees two black eyes. Two shining black eyes.

Nerea remembers her aunt as she appears in the photograph she wants to show her mother. Laughing, in the kitchen at the Izagirre Restaurant, holding onto her sister. Her hand is on Luisa's shoulder, and Luisa's head leans toward her hand. They are two but they seem like one, as if they were connected by a fine, invisible line. As if they were two limbs of the same body.

She was going to light a cigarette but, realising that there is no smoking in the airport, she puts the pack back in her purse. She doesn't feel like looking for the smokers' lounge since it will be far away somewhere. She puts the pack in her purse and when she raises her head, she feels a hand on her shoulder.

'Aunt Dolores!'

She was looking at the arrivals gate the whole time and didn't see her aunt come through. She must have flown through, she thinks, since her aunt is just like Tinker Bell in *Peter Pan*, only fifty years older. Seen from the side, her aunt looks older, but when she has her aunt's eyes right in front of her, she can see that she's as young as ever. Her shining dark eyes. They hug each other and look at each other, repeating unfinished sentences. 'And you? And you?' The question fires rapidly from both of their mouths and when Dolores opens her arms, it seems to Nerea as if she sprinkles gold dust. Tinker Bell's gold fairy dust.

Aunt Dolores' eyes never get old because while she's been living in Germany, her eyes have been in the land of her birth, awaiting her return. Only the eyes of those who stay in their native land get old, thinks Nerea. Those that see their surroundings changing every day, like her mother's eyes. The eyes of people who leave their homeland, however, stay in the land of their birth and barely get older at all while they are far from the body. Hence the sparkle in her aunt's eyes. While she was living in Germany, her eyes were here waiting for her.

'How is she?' Dolores asks without taking her hand from Nerea's shoulder.

'You'll see soon enough,' says Nerea.

'I brought the photos you asked for, and the other things,' Dolores adds, glancing at her old suitcase.

The doctor asked them to do this. It would be helpful to

get Luisa's mind to react to show her photos or similar things. Nerea thinks her aunt will have brought the picture taken in the kitchen at the Izagirre Restaurant, the twin of the one she must have at home.

With each step Dolores takes she gives a little hop, as if she wanted to escape the gravity of the earth. As they leave the parking lot, her shining black eyes stare through the window of the car as if seeking something familiar, something that would prove that she is back in her own country. But all she sees are the same brands she sees in Germany and the same billboards for the same companies. Finally, a farmhouse she spots behind a large billboard for IKEA confirms that she has arrived in her own country, the Basque Country. And she sighs.

She bites her lips and stands there, teeth on her lips. She is worried about her sister's condition. She is nervous. She blinks her eyes rapidly.

'Are you sure you don't want to stop at the house and take a shower, or leave your suitcase...?'

'No, let's go to the hospital,' she decides. She keeps blinking, while looking at all the signs on the side of the road.

Aunt Dolores' old suitcase. Made of leather. She always travels to the Basque Country with the same suitcase or one just like it. When Dolores used to come back for Christmas with Uncle Sebastian and Nerea's cousin Igone, Nerea would always stand and look at that suitcase as if there were treasure inside. And she wasn't too far wrong, because a whole life can fit in a suitcase like this one.

She asks after Igone, her cousin, Dolores' daughter. But rather than telling about Igone, Dolores talks more about Igone's son, her grandson. He has started school. He's a very smart boy but he speaks only German. Nerea doesn't know

25

him because she hasn't seen her cousin since she got married. Nerea's aunt's eyes get big when she talks about her grandson. It is their grandson who keeps Dolores and her husband in Germany. As if he were an anchor.

'Careful. Aren't you going awfully fast?'

'Don't worry, Aunt Dolores. I know how to drive.'

'Yes, you sound like your father. Paulo said the same thing to your mother and me the first time he took us in the car.' She nods but doesn't take her eyes off the road for even a moment, as if she were the one driving. 'Once, when they were engaged and your father had just gotten his licence, Paulo was driving us along the coast road. He told us to relax, he knew how to drive, like you told me just now, but he didn't look like such a good driver to us and we were terrified on that drive. Just think, I remember it like it was yesterday, that's how scared I was.'

Gesturing with her hands, Dolores tells how years later, once they were married, Paulo had confessed to Luisa that he had been afraid too on that drive, he could barely control the car on the curves. While he was telling Nerea's mother and aunt to relax, every time he went around a curve, he said to himself, 'another one down!' as if having made it around the bend successfully amazed him as well. 'Another one down!' Paulo was saying to himself while the sweat poured from his brow.

'"Another one down!" he was telling himself. And telling us to relax, the scoundrel,' says Dolores, nodding.

Nerea laughs without looking away from the road.

'Relax, Aunt Dolores. I really do know how to drive.'

Her aunt's voice calms her down. Always telling stories from the old days. Her aunt always has a story about the past to explain the present. In the face of any event, she tells about something that happened in the past and her listener feels as if the world hasn't changed at all in the last hundred years.

Ignoring her aunt's advice, Nerea maintains her speed. She feels like smoking but that might be a step too far. Then her aunt would say what was she thinking, driving with only one hand, and she would surely tell an old story about a one-armed man from the village. While Nerea is thinking this, they go around a tight curve and, as if they had rehearsed it, they both yell 'another one down!' and burst out laughing. Nerea loves laughing with her aunt. Her aunt is like a balm, like an ointment for a wound.

'How much this has changed,' her aunt murmurs as they enter the hospital.

She looks up and down, left and right. Quickly. Like the pigeons on the roof.

'Do you know when I last came to this hospital?' she asks Nerea when they get into the elevator.

'When?'

'The day you were born. How long...'

'A long time,' interrupts Nerea. 'A long time ago.'

While they watch the numbers change on the elevator, Dolores tells how Luisa had to stay in the hospital longer than usual after giving birth. Compared with Xabier's easy birth, Nerea's had been very complicated. As if Nerea didn't want to come out. As if she were afraid of the world. That's how she says it: as if she were afraid of the world. And she started being afraid of the world early on, she says. Too early, Nerea thinks.

Nerea didn't know until today that her mother had had a hard birth. This too she had hidden, like she now tries to hide the word *hospital* on the sheets. Always doing what she can to not bother others. To not worry others. Nerea would like to know what else she has hidden.

When they get to Luisa's room, the laughter they shared on the way disappears from their lips. Before going into the room where her sister lies, Dolores rubs her hands together. She is nervous. She goes in at last, and there sees an elderly woman asleep in a hospital bed. The expression on her face suggests that for a moment she barely recognises her sister. 'Luisa,' she whispers and stays by the door, as if she didn't want to get too close. Her chin trembles. Her sister looks old. After so many days in the hospital and wearing the nightgown they put on her, she looks ten years older than she is. Dolores greets the women by the window with a nod, and the younger one says to come on in, they won't wake Luisa, she's been sleeping all morning. Pili speaks to them as if they were entering her living room.

After introductions, Dolores says she has come from Germany and Pili asks where in Germany she lives, since she also has family there. When Dolores says Frankfurt, Pili says 'no, no,' shaking her head, her relatives live in a different city, but she doesn't remember the name of it. 'What was it again?' she says, and then her mother Pilar, looking out the window, says 'Hannover.' She says it as if throwing a stone: 'Hannover.' And Pili says, 'that's it, Hannover,' that's where her uncle and...

Nerea and her aunt are waiting for the downpour of words to stop so they can give Luisa their full attention, and they just stare at Pili, dizzy with all the words, until she says, 'she's awake.' Again a sparkling piece of gold appears among the stones of the creek. They realise she means Luisa and they both look over at her bed. And there they see her, eyes open, aware.

Dolores goes over to her slowly. Nerea follows her aunt. Dolores approaches her sister so slowly, Nerea thinks she might as well be walking all the distance from Germany to the Basque Country.

'Luisa,' says Dolores when she reaches the side of the bed. She says nothing else, just takes her sister's hand. Her aunt says her mother's name so sweetly it makes Nerea shiver all the way down to the tips of her toes.

Luisa is looking at Dolores. She looks at her sister's young eyes that waited for her in the Basque Country. Seeing the two sisters holding hands, Nerea feels like time has stopped or perhaps time has gone backwards, and the two women before her have stepped out of the photograph of the kitchen of the Izagirre Restaurant to meet these many years later in a white hospital room. And for a moment she sees them in black and white. Holding onto each other, as in the photo. Bound by a fine thread, as they were then.

Luisa licks her lips. Everyone falls silent and when Nerea swallows hard, she thinks everyone in the room must be able to hear it.

And then it happens: Luisa speaks at last. Nerea hears her mother's voice, which she has been unable to recall until now.

'Dolores,' she says with a smile. And, weighing that word, Nerea thinks it must weigh a kilo. A two-pounder, as her aunt would say.

She recognises her. She recognises her sister. Dolores is the first person she's recognised. And it's the first time since she's been in the hospital that Nerea has heard her mother's voice. Nerea feels like the veins in her neck are about to explode when she hears this voice that her mother summons from deep inside her. Dolores. A two-pound word. Then Luisa turns her head to look at Nerea and Nerea silently says her own name to herself again and again: 'Nerea, Nerea, Nerea,' as if by repeating her name she could build a bridge between the two of them. A bridge made of names. But her mother says nothing, she doesn't recognise her, and she looks at Dolores again.

'Dolores,' her mother says again, swallowing hard, furrowing her brow. 'But where are you going to sleep?' She looks worried.

Everyone falls silent. And with the silence, the blank smile returns to Luisa's face. She stares at the wall across from her, lost in her smile. And Nerea feels again that something has gotten away from her the way the string of a helium balloon slips through the fingers.

Dolores goes out of the room. She leaves without saying anything, almost at a run. She doesn't want to cry in front of anybody else. It is Nerea who holds her mother's hand then and, suddenly, it seems as if her mother has returned to awareness. It is the first time she has spoken directly to her. But it seems as if she is talking not to Nerea but to Dolores.

'When will we go?' Nerea's mother asks.

'Where?' Nerea answers nervously, startled. And her question is a hook, to pull her mother's words from the cave where she has hidden them.

'To the lighthouse.'

And with that, she has run out of strength, as if forcing the words out from deep within has taken a tremendous effort. Her gaze is lost in the distance again. Then Nerea thinks her mother really is very confused and just repeats what she's heard around her. Nevertheless, she noticed something different in the way her mother said she wanted to go to the lighthouse. A look she had never seen in her mother before. Not since she's been in the hospital, nor before that either.

Her eyes were fluttering and made Nerea think of the sparkle in her aunt's eyes.

Nerea lets her breath out. She doesn't understand her mother's words, but she's glad she spoke. A crack has opened in the stone wall between her mother and the world, and she is sure it is thanks to the sparkle in Aunt Dolores' eyes. On the white wall of the hospital room, a ray of light falls from a narrow crack. A ray of hope that Dolores' eyes have brought. Tinker Bell flies into the room. The golden trail of her fairy dust can still be seen on the white walls.

6

'Who the hell is stealing the flowers? Who?'

Bittori enters the kitchen at the Izagirre Restaurant with a shout, carrying the vase from the counter in her hands. Luisa hides the novel in her hands under her apron, since Bittori has forbidden her from reading in the kitchen. She and Dolores shrug their shoulders to show they know nothing about it, and both of them start peeling potatoes.

Bittori buys flowers from the farmer's wife who stops by the restaurant every Thursday, and sets them on the counter in a glass vase, convinced it gives the restaurant a bit of class. But lately, every now and then, a single flower will be missing from a bouquet and Bittori suspects the young girls from the kitchen.

Bittori returns the vase to the counter angrily and rearranges the flowers that remain so that no one will be able to tell some are missing. Once Bittori leaves the kitchen, Luisa sighs and waits for the best time to claim she has errands to run so she can escape to the lighthouse.

7

Fidel's voice. As unpleasant as the smell of the aftershave he uses. Over the years it has become bitter. As has he.

'How's your mother?' Fidel asks Nerea as he approaches her desk.

Ever since he was named editor-in-chief, his voice and everything about him have changed, Nerea thinks, and he even walks differently through the editorial office, as if he took a deep breath but didn't release it. Head high, eyebrows raised, he walks like a teacher supervising an exam. Nerea remembers the day Fidel started at the newspaper as an intern. How he entered with his head bowed, ready to do anything. And now he's getting above himself, walking from one desk to the next in the editorial office, checking to make sure everyone is doing everything right. Even the way he sits in his office chair has changed. Before, he sat on only half of his rear, ready to leap up at any moment, but now he flings his body carelessly onto his seat like a king sitting on his throne. If she hadn't known him since he was an intern, Nerea would have thought she should be grateful for him coming over to ask about her mother, but she knows him too well, and she knows that with his question he is reminding her that regardless of how her mother is, she's been putting in fewer hours at the newspaper lately.

'Well,' Nerea answers, 'she's doing all right.'

And when she hears herself say that her mother's doing 'all right,' she wonders what is right about how she's doing. Yesterday she spoke to them a little, but then her mind wandered again like a mobile without signal. She lives in her own world. In Neverland.

Nerea started working for the newspaper more than ten years ago and since that time has passed through almost all of the departments. She often thinks that the only thing left is horoscopes, and then she will truly be able to say that she has worked in all the departments. Time will tell. Thank God she left politics behind a long time ago. In that department, she was afraid she would someday have to write a story about Karlos. That was her nightmare. She imagined herself writing his name on the computer screen: Karlos Lizarribar. Writing under a picture of him, *Karlos Lizarribar, alleged perpetrator of the attack* or *Karlos Lizarribar arrested*, and just the thought of it tied her stomach in knots.

Now she writes for the Society page and while she has her ups and downs with Fidel on certain issues, such as when she remembers the direction the newspaper is taking, she writes the news more calmly now than ever before. At least she won't have to write Karlos' name on her screen.

In all the years she has worked at the newspaper, her greatest humiliations have been in the last one, always at Fidel's hands. At Fidel's bitter hands. When he comes over to her with a page in one hand and his red marker in the other, she cannot hide her revulsion. He suggests more and more changes to her articles and Nerea can feel the veins in her neck throbbing as she says she does not agree to those changes, that's not the way things are, and Fidel responds with 'you do know where you work, don't you?' Nerea would like to retort that he left his professional ethics in an ashtray on the table in one of his meetings with the bosses, and that's the only reason he is where he is today, because he left his dignity in the ashtray. Fidel has adapted perfectly to the current rules of journalism. She would love to say all that to him, but she holds her tongue.

Today, however, something explodes inside her. After the question about her mother, Fidel suggests that she completely change the title of the article she wrote, which would completely change the whole point of the article and completely invalidate everything in it.

'No, that's not possible,' says Nerea. 'Not the title.'

'We can't publish it the way it is, and you know it,' says Fidel, raising his eyebrows and tapping the top of the page with his fingers.

The article is about the different linguistic models in the educational system. Nerea wrote the report based on data from the Department of Education. The title Fidel is suggesting changes the whole meaning and point of the article.

'Then take my name off of it. Do whatever you want with the article, but take my...' Before she finishes the sentence, her phone rings. It is Aunt Dolores. The doctor wants to meet with them in an hour to discuss the results of the latest tests.

She turns off her computer while Fidel watches, and angrily says she has to go, without further explanation. Fidel follows her to the elevator. Having Fidel tagging along after her brings to mind an image from American films: people running back and forth in the corridors of a large editorial office, some speaking to others with their papers in their hands, without looking at each other. But this is neither the *Wall Street Journal* nor the *Washington Post*, and the man following her does not look like a Hollywood actor. Neither do I, thinks Nerea.

They stop in front of the elevator, Nerea waiting, Fidel talking.

'Look, Nerea, I understand you're going through a tough time right now and, I don't know, if you want to take a leave of absence...' When she hears the words *leave of absence* she feels a fire flare up in her belly and she glares at him. Nerea knows that she isn't a convenient person for Fidel to have in the office. She is one of the few who knew him when he was an intern, and she sometimes thinks when she talks to him that Fidel sees in her eyes the reflection of the intern he was, and he doesn't like it one bit. He would take any opportunity to get rid of her. A leave of absence. He would jump at the slightest excuse to fire her from the newspaper.

'Goodbye,' Nerea interrupts him, and before she gets into the elevator she turns and looks him straight in the eye. 'Remember, I don't want to see my name on that article. Put "Press Agency" or whatever you want,' she says. And she thinks if she had raised her finger as she said it, her words would have been even more forceful, but she doesn't dare go quite so far. She is shocked anyway that she has dared to say that much to Fidel. Never before has she spoken to him like this. The situation with her mother must really be getting to her.

In the ten minutes since she got in the car, she has not advanced more than twenty yards. She is trapped in a long line of cars. She called her husband to tell him she was on her way to the hospital. He said to take it easy, and to let him know if she was going to be home late. Every time the red brake light of the car in front of her goes on, she bites her lip and blows out her breath. Horrible traffic. She will be late to the doctor. That's all she needed.

A fire in her belly she thought had been extinguished was lit again by Fidel. Sometimes she asks herself what the hell she's doing working at the newspaper, busting a gut to get herself here or there, only to have some half-arsed jerk like Fidel fuck it all up later, or, even without Fidel, to put all her energy in vain into an article that very few will read. She puts a lot of effort into work that's only valid for a few hours. All of the work she does on one day is gone with the wind the next. It's frustrating. She still doesn't know if she even likes the job.

She puts out the cigarette she's holding in the ashtray and arrives at the hospital with a car full of smoke. It looks as if she has a cloud in the car, and when she gets out, the cloud follows behind her, like a bride's veil. But around the car there is no one clapping, smiling, cheering for the bride. A man on crutches, a pregnant woman, an old man holding onto his daughter's arm. That's who she sees going in and out of the hospital doors.

'She'll be here soon,' Dolores is saying to the doctor, who is sitting behind a huge desk.

Nerea begs their pardon, without mentioning the reason for her tardiness. She doesn't feel like explaining.

The doctor puts his hands together on the desk, and says 'let's see,' by way of starting the conversation. Nerea detests people who start talking by saying 'let's see.' Apparently they think that others live blindly in the dark until they speak. The doctor dresses up what he says next in scientific terminology and, using the technical words as boxing gloves, starts to punch the two women in the stomach. Briefly, the doctor tells them that before Nerea's mother got lost on the streets, there must surely have been something going on in her mind, something that suddenly exploded on her. If they had noticed something earlier, that would have been a different matter. It's too bad they didn't become aware of her illness earlier, because it would have been a different matter if they had caught it early on. Her mother's clock has fallen behind, the doctor says, using this metaphor when he runs out of scientific words. But that's just a theory, and it remains to be seen how her illness actually progresses. Four, three, two, one, zero. Nerea and her aunt are KO'd.

The doctor fiddles with the glasses in his hands as he explains things to them. Now he's lifting them up, now he brings them down. As if they were a baton. And as she watches this white-coated orchestra conductor, Nerea remembers the melody of the song her mother used to sing to her at bedtime when she was little. All of a sudden, with the sound of the bass drum in the orchestra, her world turns upside down. She imagines her mother in bed, in her house and Lewis', sleeping with Maialen, and she is now the one who sings the song and strokes the forehead of her mother. It seems to her that her mother has become her daughter overnight and her head sinks a few centimeters, so heavy is the weight she feels upon her shoulders.

She leaves the meeting and stops in the hallway with her aunt. She can't forget the doctor's words: 'If we had known earlier…' Nerea had suspected something earlier, but hadn't said anything. Like a child, she had stuck her fingers in her ears. And now she drags the weight of guilt from the hospital home, from home to the editorial office, and from the office back to the hospital. Leaving a dark trail on her way. A trail darker than the dark blue worn by fishermen.

'Do you want a coffee?' her aunt asks her.

'With a little milk,' she answers, without looking her in the eye.

As they stand in front of the coffee machine, she sees Pili approaching down the hall and, while taking little sips of her coffee, thinks where the hell did that woman pull that name from, Herman.

The coffee gives her a stomach ache. It is even more bitter than Fidel's aftershave. Acrid. She throws it in the trash after drinking only half, greets Pili as she passes by, and heads for the restroom. She carries a pack of cigarettes in her hand.

8

The six women are smiling at the camera, looking up. Showing their black and white smiles. The photograph was taken from above, as if the photographer had climbed up on the kitchen table. In the kitchen of the Izagirre Restaurant are the sisters Luisa and Dolores, their mother Petra, their Aunt Bittori, and two other girls who helped with the work in the kitchen. *1951. Izagirre Restaurant* reads Nerea in the black ink on the reverse side.

The photo was taken in the early years of the Izagirre Restaurant, three years after it went from lemonade factory to restaurant. Because before it became a restaurant, it had been a lemonade factory. *Izagirre Sodas*. Luis Izagirre, Luisa and Dolores' father, made lemonade and sold it, and also wine, in the town. Many of the men who lived in the town would bring a snack from home and go there to drink a glass of wine and, with some tables and chairs set out, the lemonade shop became a bar. Not long after, they put in a small kitchen and started serving afternoon snacks and little by little, it turned into a restaurant. It went from *Izagirre Sodas* to *Izagirre Restaurant*. However, the lemonade factory never entirely disappeared because Luis Izagirre kept making lemonade in the back of the building, next to the storehouse.

Like a bouquet of flowers, the women who worked in the kitchen are arranged in a circle. Right in the middle, at the top, is Bittori, young Luisa and Dolores' aunt, their mother's sister. She resembles the queen in *Alice in Wonderland*. Chin up, shoulders back, white hair in a ponytail. She looks at the camera defiantly. After spending her whole youth as a servant in a mansion in Bilbao, she returned to the town without a husband, when she was too old to be married. Bittori was the leader and director of the kitchen at the Izagirre Restaurant, and she looks at the camera with the gaze of a leader. As if she were saying, 'Here am I and here are my girls.'

Behind her an old radio can be seen, near the ladles and cooking pots hung on the wall. When she sees the radio, Nerea remembers a story she has heard her aunt tell many times. She used to tell it when she came from Germany for her Christmas visit. It's one of her classics. Bittori always had the radio on in the kitchen because she really liked to hear people talking in Spanish. One day, Dolores went into the kitchen and realised that they were talking about Franco on the radio. She asked Bittori what they were saying, and she said that Franco wasn't well, he must be ill since they kept talking on the radio about his dietary regime. Over and over they said it, Franco's regime this, Franco's regime that. And, the way Aunt Dolores told it, Bittori put her hand to her mouth and whispered that he would surely die soon. And then she warned her not to tell anyone, because you never know, and 'Lazarus rose from the dead, after all!' Nerea remembers how her aunt used to laugh when she told this story, and she smiles a little too.

Bittori is serious in the photograph. Proud. Here am I and

here are my girls. Nerea had heard her aunt say that the years Bittori had spent abroad had given her this natural authority. She went around wanting to show how much she had learned in her years as a servant in the mansion in Bilbao. Whenever foreigners came to the restaurant, she would leave her apron in the kitchen and she herself would go out to serve them. Regardless of whether they were English or French, she would speak to them in Spanish, very slowly and pronouncing each word carefully: 'There is tu-na in to-ma-to sauce.' Bittori truly believed she was speaking English or French, and would return proudly to the kitchen, mumbling that who knows what would happen if she weren't there at the restaurant. Luisa and Dolores used to call her the kitchen philosopher, because she loved to talk about the ups and downs of life, always ending with 'Now we've seen it all!'

Luisa and Dolores are united in a hug in the photograph. Nerea sees Dolores' young eyes and remembers them as she saw them at the airport. Dolores has raised her eyebrows high and has her left arm around her sister. Luisa is also smiling. She has long dark hair, which she wears in a braid. When she sees her mother's face, Nerea remembers a photograph from her own youth. A photo taken at the Urkiola campsite with Karlos, in which she appears with Blackie.

She takes a sip of her morning coffee and her aunt appears behind her.

'Beautiful girls, huh?' she says. She is already dressed in her street clothes. Since she has been in the house, Nerea has never once seen her in a nightdress or pyjamas. She sees her going into her room fully clothed, and coming out fully clothed. She suspects Dolores may sleep fully clothed.

She serves her aunt coffee, and tells her to sit down. Setting her cup of coffee on the table, Nerea is looking at her aunt's expression as she stares at the old photo. Dolores furrows her brow and seems to be looking beyond the photograph.

'It was about that time that your mother started waiting tables. She didn't like it; she liked running errands instead. She'd take the old bike and, on the pretense of running errands, she'd take a little detour to the coast. To smell the sea, as she said. But even though she didn't like waiting tables, Bittori would order her to do it to get rid of her shyness once and for all. "See if you can shake off your shyness, girl!" she would say. That's how your mother met your father: waiting tables. Paolo often came to the restaurant for lunch, but we knew it was really to see your mother. Bittori would send her to serve him. She always ordered her to put the vase that was on the bar on your father's table. "Take it to him, girl, and at least smile at him!" she would tell your mother. She approved of that young man for your mother.'

Maialen calls from her room.

'I'll go,' says Dolores.

And soon Nerea hears the child's laughter. Maialen is bursting with laughter. She doesn't laugh this hard even at television cartoons. No doubt Dolores is telling her a story about the old days.

It's Sunday. And Nerea loves Sundays, or at least she does when she doesn't have to go to work, because she often has to work on Sundays as well. They are the worst days of the week then, since while she's at the office she keeps thinking that Maialen doesn't have to go to school and if it weren't for work, she would be spending the day with her and with Lewis. But today she doesn't have to work. She'll have breakfast and go to the hospital. Today is a nice calm Sunday, at least that's what Nerea thinks. But soon all calm will abandon her. When she goes down to the street and gets into her car with the plump Sunday newspaper in her hands, her calm will fly out through the air vents when she sees that the previous day's article is signed with her name but the headline is Fidel's. She flings the paper to the floor, where it ends up open and strewn about the footwell. She stomps on the gas and peels out for the hospital.

9

On the pretense of running an errand, young Luisa takes the bicycle and escapes to the lighthouse, as she often does. With her eyes on the horizon where the sea ends, she breathes in deeply. Then she closes her eyes, the better to smell the salt water. She hears the crash of the waves hitting the rocks, and then the gush of the water. She throws her head back and puts her hand in her open collar. She takes out a flower. She opens her eyes, smells the flower and, at the moment when the wind blows the strongest, throws it in the water. And then she shouts a name out loud, looking to the northeast. Looking toward where the Urkiolamendi is fishing.

10

Even if she doesn't want to admit it, she has been waiting. She is waiting. Knowing that it had to happen some day, she is waiting. Nerea has always known that one day she would have news of Karlos. Even if she doesn't want to admit it, she has always known that that day would come. Because those who have disappeared reappear eventually. One way or another, they reappear. She has been waiting like a fisherman's wife when the ship goes down. She wants news, but at the same time, she doesn't want to hear. And one day, one way or another, the news arrives. One day flotsam appears at the water's edge on the beach. And that flotsam puts an end to all questions. Because the shirt the water brought is her husband's. A dark blue shirt.

'Shouldn't you pick up these newspaper pages?' says Aunt Dolores when she gets in the car. They got up early to go to the hospital, and her aunt finds the newspaper she flung down the night before under her feet.

'Yes, Aunt Dolores. Later,' answers Nerea and steps on the gas to go up the garage ramp.

She used to answer her mother the same way. 'Yes, Mum. Later,' she said when she was young, when her mother told her to clean her room. Ever since her mother has been in the hospital, Nerea has remembered several interactions with her, and in all of them she sees herself answering back without thinking, and this pains her. Now she would be ready to do anything her mother asks of her, but it is her mother who is not ready. As she has over the last several days, Nerea wonders where her mother's mind is wandering. Where has it gone, the shyness of the young girl who used to serve food at the Izagirre Restaurant? Where is the tenderness of the mother who used to stroke her forehead at night? Where is the smile of the woman who used to listen to her sister's stories? Where are all those things now? She sees them covered with a sheet, in a white and misty place.

Her appointment book for today is filled with notes written in blue pen. Two press conferences and an interview for the weekend report, among other things. And she hates days like this.

'And what sorts of things does Lewis translate? What's he working on now, for example?' asks Dolores, no doubt to break the silence that fills the car.

'He's translating a biography at the moment, but he does all different kinds of work. A lot of times they're technical texts, those are the most boring ones. But now he's doing a biography.'

This question is her aunt's way of asking if everything is okay with Lewis. She wants to raise the topic of Lewis. At dinner, Lewis leaves the kitchen as soon as possible, using work as an excuse, and Dolores wants to know if it's always like that or if it's because she is there. She always sees Lewis retreating. She wants to know if the English are like that, or if there is some problem between them. But they soon drop the topic of Lewis, because they arrive at the hospital.

When they go into Luisa's room, Pili gives them the daily report. Luisa slept well and didn't talk in her sleep like she did the day before. When Pili says this, Nerea immediately realises that she hasn't told her aunt anything about that. Dolores, startled, interrupts.

'But when did she speak? Did she talk in her sleep?'

Pili says yes and looks at Nerea. Yes, she did tell Nerea, did she not mention anything? The two women turn to look at Nerea, as if waiting for an answer, and at that moment the phone that she carries in her purse starts ringing. 'Excuse me,' says Nerea, and goes out. The last words she hears as the door closes are Pili's: 'Yes, it was as if she were calling for someone. What was the name again?'

Nerea leans against the wall in the hallway, phone to her ear. It is her friend Maite on the other end of the line. When she hears her voice, it seems like more light comes in the window, and she looks at the plant next to the window. It has very long, green leaves. She remembers the flowers Bittori used to put on the bar in the restaurant. Maite gives her strength. Just as she startled everyone in that Oxford pub with the shriek she let out, she is equally capable with her strong voice of cheering anyone up.

'How's everything going?' asks Maite.

Maite repeats the offer she made on the day Nerea told her what had happened to her mother: that she can spend a couple hours at the hospital whenever Nerea wants, when Nerea can't be there.

'It's okay, Aunt Dolores is here.'

'The one from Germany?'

'Yes. Thank goodness for her. And Mum recognised her. She said her name when she saw her.'

'Really? That's a very good sign, Nerea. Wow, I'm glad...

Listen, what's your schedule like? Can we get together for a meal? For lunch? We need to talk.'

'What is it?'

'Nothing, it's nothing. So can we get together?'

'I don't know. From here I have to go straight to a press conference, without even stopping in at the office.'

'Where's the press conference?'

They make a lunch date in the end. Just for a quick bite because today Nerea is on a tight schedule. Thank goodness Maialen eats lunch at school. Nerea leaves the press conference and runs to the restaurant. She hasn't had the chance to see Maite for a long time. Between work and her mother, she doesn't even have time to see friends. She must be having a problem with Iñaki, thinks Nerea, and needs to talk about it. She hasn't been well lately. They haven't moved on since they found out they can't have children. Maite has been putting on weight ever since because of anxiety.

'And what's Lewis up to?' she asks once they're at their table in the restaurant, waiting for their food. Apparently everyone has to ask her about Lewis today.

'Good. Good. He's at home.'

'Yeah. What about you?'

'Well, I won't lie to you. I'm a bit dazed.'

She confesses that she has had almost no chance to talk to anyone since her mother's problem started, and she feels like she's being cut with thorns.

'I don't know, Maite. I'd like to stop the clock sometimes. There aren't enough hours in the day. I go from the office to the hospital, from the hospital back to the office... And then when I get home I'm exhausted, and often by the time I get there, my daughter is asleep. And the whole time I'm thinking that I'm missing a precious piece of life, that someone has

49

stolen a piece of life from me. I don't know, before I was just barely getting by too, not quite getting to everything, but with this thing with my mother, everything is upside down. Everything is difficult, Maite. Suddenly everything is difficult.'

She takes a cigarette and her lighter out of the pack of cigarettes and lights up. She takes a drag, then goes on. Maite looks at her with compassion.

'…and with Lewis, well, lately I don't know what's happening to us. In the evening, we say about four words to each other before we fall asleep. We tell each other about our day, but nothing else. We have nothing else to give each other. We spend the whole day apart, and then, when we get together, it seems like we have nothing to talk about.'

'Take it easy, Nere. That's normal. It's not an easy situation, but you'll see. Everything will work out when your mother gets better and comes home.'

'Whose home will she go to though? Hers? Ours?'

Nerea sighs and takes a long drag on her cigarette. Maite furrows her brow. As if a thread inside were being tightened.

They fall silent for a moment. The waiter brings the first course and Nerea stubs out her cigarette in the ashtray. Then, when she passes that hand across her forehead, she smells cigarette on her fingers, and she remembers the yellowed fingers of old smokers. The image disgusts her.

'I only have twenty-five minutes left,' she tells Maite after looking at the clock. She is hoping Maite will get to the point; she wants to know why she called her. But Maite doesn't seem to understand. Or doesn't want to.

'Aren't you going to eat your chips?' asks Maite, with her fork in her hand. She raises it up and Nerea thinks she looks like Neptune rising from the sea. All she needs is a beard.

'No, I'm full, I'm not hungry.'

'You need to eat more,' she says, and sticks her fork into the little mountain of chips Nerea left on one side of her plate. Neptune has gone fishing. Mouth full, Maite keeps talking. 'Well, to tell the truth, Lewis has never been a big talker, has he?'

She seems to be in no hurry to get to the point. It's odd, because Maite has never been one for beating around the bush. She usually goes straight to the point the way her fork went to the chips. Today, however, she's taking the long way around. Nerea waits. She wants to know the real reason why Maite called her.

'So… How's everything with you, Maite?'

'Well…' She makes an effort to start the sentence but then seems to change her mind.

Nerea thinks that something really serious must be going on, that she must have a problem and can't figure out what to do about it.

'How are things with Iñaki? Are you having problems?'

'No. It's not about Iñaki.' She falls silent for a second. 'It's Karlos.'

When she hears Karlos' name, Nerea's face stiffens. She is caught from behind by a big wave. The wave breaks over her and spins her around and around all the way to the beach. On the way she keeps swallowing water. Her eyes are wide and her brow furrowed. It has been a long time since anyone has mentioned that name in her presence. Karlos. Why is Maite bringing up this old story now? And then she understands. The moment, then, has come. The sea has finally brought some flotsam to the water's edge on the beach. And she is there waiting. She wants to see what has turned up, but at the same time, like the fisherman's wife, she doesn't want to see.

'I should have told you before but I didn't know where to start. They've seen Karlos in town. I didn't know whether to tell you or not, what with your mother and all, but then I thought it would be better to tell you. Because otherwise, if you didn't know anything and then ran into each other on the street, you'd have a heart attack.'

'Where did they see him?' Nerea asks, and realises that her voice has come out huskier than usual. She couldn't speak from her throat; her voice came from her gut.

'Here, in town.'

'But could he really be here? Why did he come?' Nerea feels like her eyes are going to pop right out of her head.

'I don't know for sure what the story is, but, according to what I heard, the statute of limitations has passed on the arrest orders against him after so many years. But I could be wrong.'

Her cigarette is about to burn her fingers. The twenty-five minutes she mentioned earlier have long since passed but Nerea doesn't get up from the table. She is no longer in a hurry. Her vision blurs and she remembers a scene from fifteen years ago. She sees images from the last day she saw Karlos. They are standing outside the door at her parents' house. Karlos says they won't see each other the next day because he has to go to Hendaia for a dental appointment. And then he kisses her. A quavering kiss. Then Nerea says 'don't be chicken.' If going to the dentist does this to him, he's done for. 'Thank goodness you don't have to give birth,' she says. She laughs, puts her key in the lock, doesn't look back to see Karlos moving away down the rainy street. Because she doesn't know that Karlos has started a journey that goes down this street, because she doesn't know that she won't see him again for years or maybe ever. She doesn't know that the young man setting off down the street will become a ghost that will appear over and over again in her nightmares. Karlos Lizarribar, the alleged perpetrator. If she had known, she would have run after him and grabbed his shoulders and begged him not to go.

From that day on, Nerea had a black look to her. She couldn't wipe the bitter expression off her face until she met Lewis in Oxford two years later. But even after she got together with Lewis, her worries about Karlos churned around and around inside her head for years, and then there was the pain that he left in her gut, and her anger, and her feeling of emptiness. Why hadn't he told her anything? She didn't even have the chance to say goodbye to him properly. *Don't be chicken*. Those were her last words to him, thinking he was going to the dentist. *Don't be chicken*. And that last sentence has come back to her in a million nightmares. It wasn't exactly a fraught and laden final sentence like in the movies. *Don't be chicken*. At life's most important moments we say trivial sentences like that, she thinks. Ever since she said goodbye to him with that trivial sentence, Karlos has always been on her mind, a constant worry. At the most important milestones of her life too, his face comes to her and she wonders if news of her ever reaches him. Does he know she's married? Does he know she has a daughter? Does he know...? And even though it's hard for her to admit it, before all of the most important decisions she has had to make in recent years, Karlos comes to her mind, and she wonders what he would think about the decision she has made.

'Don't you have to go to work? You're going to be late,' says Maite, rousing her from her daydream.

She nods, and then asks, 'Who saw him? Iñaki?'

'No, Iñaki's cousin Martin,' says Maite, and bows her head.

'And did they speak?'

'A couple of words, I think,' she sighs. 'After fifteen years, a couple of words.'

Nerea has crumpled up the empty cigarette pack she was holding. Completely. She wonders whether Karlos would ask the friends he runs into about her, but she doesn't mention it to Maite. She would like to know. And she doesn't want to know.

They go out of the bar and she tosses the crumpled cigarette pack into a bin a yard from the door, like a basketball player. The pack hits the side and falls to the pavement.

'Shit,' she mumbles, and thinks that Bittori was right – *Lazarus rose from the dead, after all!* – and that there is never any peace to be had.

11

She sees Fidel from afar, inside his glass-walled office, talking on the phone. Her idea had been to go straight in, but she thinks it will be better to go in when he's finished. She doesn't want to wait by his door. She wants to burst in on him, having built up speed. In the meantime, she puts the cassette and notebook she used in the morning press conference on her desk and turns on the computer. *Whirrrrr*. She would like to be able to turn her head on and off when she wants, like a computer.

At the moment she would like to turn it off. She has too many things on her mind, too many images one on top of another: she sees her mother lying in the hospital bed, Fidel in his glass-walled office, and Karlos. Karlos' image has intruded on all the others. She always knew the day would come when she would have news of him. But it has arrived at the worst possible moment. She doesn't want to see him. Not now. But even if she doesn't want to see him, she can't get her questions about Karlos out of her mind. How is he? What does he look like? Has he aged? She thinks he must have aged after having been on the run for so many years. Has he got a woman by his side? Does she still hold a place in his heart?

Karlos' life, like the computer, goes *whirrrrr*. After being off for so many years, it has been turned on. But perhaps with an outdated program.

She remembers Karlos' eyes, and how his gaze trembled one summer night. He had looked at her so shyly before that first kiss. Nerea finds it hard to believe that the person who was shy of giving her a tremulous kiss is now the one who appears to her as a ghost. She remembers his hands. They were sweaty. How much those hands must have sweated since he disappeared from town, she thinks. How many cold sweats. She makes an effort to remember the words Karlos said to her on the beach and for a moment it seems like she hears his voice. But the voice that reaches her ears is a different one. Fidel's. Putting his jacket on, he walks right past Nerea on his way out.

'Santi's in charge. Ask him how much space each of you gets,' says Fidel, and runs out.

And likewise, all the words that Nerea wants to say to Fidel also run away. Fly away. Turned into steam.

The telephone. It's her aunt. She has been waiting for this call all afternoon, because the doctor was supposed to stop by and see her mother but after talking with Maite, she had almost forgotten.

'How is she?'

'Fine. The doctor said we shouldn't worry. She needs time, but little by little, she'll definitely start recognising people. We all have to help her. We have to help her remember who she is.'

'I'll come pick you up, Aunt Dolores, when I'm done here. But I don't know what time that'll be.'

They will have to help her mother remember who she is. These are not reassuring words. Nerea wonders for the millionth time where her mother is, while she stares at the blue screen before her eyes. And she thinks she might be in the kitchen of the Izagirre Restaurant, peeling potatoes; or on a highway full of curves in a car that her father is driving; or cupping a little girl's chin in her hand, saying 'raise your head, Nerea'; or in a world Nerea doesn't even know, calling to an unknown man named Herman, for example.

The hubbub coming from the politics department rouses her. Something has happened. Something serious. She hears a co-worker walking past say that a car was blown up. And she closes her ears. She doesn't want to hear anything else. She doesn't want to know where it was, she doesn't want to know against whom it was. The weight she was carrying on her shoulders is heavier now. Karlos, Mum, Fidel... and now this car, this explosion, the smoke and fire she can well imagine. She would like to escape sometimes. To somewhere far away.

Today she will leave the paper early, since the directorship has taken one society page away from them so that the politics reporters can tell all about the explosion. They will need more pages so they can include photos of the exploded car, infographics about the location, and politicians' declarations. They will need extra space especially for the politicians' declarations, she thinks. To put in the usual words. Empty words. And it happens just as she thinks it will. She leaves the office earlier than ever. What had been a full-page report in the morning was reduced to a column.

She picks her aunt up from the hospital and, as they're driving, waits for her question. She thinks Dolores will ask her why she didn't tell her that her mother talked in her sleep, but her aunt doesn't even mention it.

'We need to think about where we'll be taking her when she gets out of the hospital,' says Dolores.

They have to think about where her mother will live. The way she is now, she can't live alone, as she has until now. As long as she's in the hospital, they can take care of things pretty well, especially with Pili there. She stays there every night and, while Nerea still thinks her voice sounds like bagpipes, it sounds sweeter and sweeter to her. She helps them out a lot. Knowing that she'll be there, they can go home and relax at night.

Seeing that Dolores is not going to bring up the previous day, Nerea herself explains.

'I meant to tell you that Mum was talking in her sleep and all, but it slipped my mind. I'm sorry,' she says.

Dolores nods, but remains silent.

'What did Pili tell you, Aunt Dolores?'

'Just that. The same thing she told you. That she's been talking. In her sleep.'

'Did she tell you she's been mentioning someone's name?'

'Yes, she told me.'

'And?'

'And what?'

'She told you she's been mentioning the name Herman?'

'Yes, she told me.'

'Did Mum know a Herman then?'

'Yes.'

'And?'

'And what?' her aunt answers. She has never spoken to her in that tone of voice before. It sounds to Nerea like an axe chopping into a stump. Dolores wanted to cut off the conversation like an axe.

'I'd just like to know who he was, that's all...' says Nerea quietly.

'Well, it's a very long story, I'll tell you another time,' says her aunt, lowering her voice without raising her eyes from the road.

'Aunt Dolores...' pleads Nerea. And her voice now is the one she used to use to plead with her aunt as a child to show her what was in her suitcase.

Nerea's aunt has surprised her. Dolores has always been willing to tell any story, especially when it's a story about the old days. It's her speciality, just like Bittori's specialty was tuna in tomato sauce. Now, however, she doesn't want to give out any information. She's avoiding the topic. Nevertheless, just when Nerea thinks she won't say any more, she picks up the conversation again. Her gaze is lost in the lights along the road, and she speaks as if she weren't in the car. As if from far away.

'A similar thing happens when you paint an old wardrobe, for example.' She falls silent for a moment, and Nerea doesn't say a word; she just waits to see where this will lead. 'Think about what happens when you put a new coat of paint over the old one on a wardrobe. Brown paint over white, for example. Well, after a while you think the wardrobe was always brown. You forget that it was ever white. But over the years, the wardrobe suffers from humidity, heat, cold, the touches of many hands, and because of all these things, a piece of the top layer flakes off. A little piece of paint flakes off and under the brown, you see that the wardrobe has a white coat. At first you're surprised, but then you say, "that's right, it's true, this wardrobe was white once." This is what happens with us too. We repaint ourselves endlessly, putting one event on top of another, forgetting the one underneath or thinking that we've forgotten. But one day we take a hit and, just like the wardrobe, little pieces of the top layer fall to the ground, and other layers can then be seen, earlier ones.

And then we say, "yes, that's right, this wardrobe was white once."'

Nerea is reminded of Bittori. Dolores sounds like the philosopher of the kitchen. She says Luisa's colours from long ago are starting to show, and images, names, people that she thought had disappeared are now returning to her. Like Herman. Dolores lowers her voice as if it makes her sad to remember these things from so long ago.

'Who was he, an old boyfriend of Mum's?' Nerea asks.

'Yes. You never knew anything about him, did you?'

Nerea shakes her head. Dolores sniffs and huffs. She can't believe it. How can Herman's name have come up now, after so many years? After so many years, she repeats. She squints her eyes, as if she had to make an extra effort since what she wants to remember is so far away. And she starts huffing again, as if she just can't believe it.

Nerea wants to ask a thousand questions. A thousand and one. But she doesn't know where to begin, and now they are home. As they go up in the elevator, she tries to imagine her mother at age twenty, laughing with an unknown boy, holding hands, and she feels uneasy. As if her mother were doing something bad.

They go into her daughter's room and find Lewis sitting on the edge of the bed telling Maialen stories about Alice. Alice has fallen into her Wonderland. Suddenly she has found herself living in a new world and she doesn't know its laws. She didn't ask to be there, but there she is, and she'll just have to get used to it.

'And Alice wonders if sometimes things go back to being as they once were. She doesn't understand how things work in this new world,' Lewis explains to Maialen.

'But why doesn't she just climb out of the hole?' Maialen asks.

'She'd like to, but she doesn't know how,' answers Lewis.

Nerea strokes her daughter's hair and kisses her forehead. 'Time to go to sleep.'

'When will Grandma come?' asks Maialen.

'Soon. She'll be here by Christmas. She'll come with Father Christmas,' says Nerea. 'And she'll bring you a big present.'

And she kisses her forehead again.

While Lewis is brushing his teeth in the bathroom, Nerea sits on the bed with the box of photos she took from the wardrobe. She has to choose which ones to show her mother. As she sits there with the black and white photos, she wonders if there are any pictures of her mother and Herman together. If so, her mother would have hidden the photographs. She turns over the box of photos and the dust makes her sneeze. Lewis' voice comes from the bathroom, saying 'bless you.' And Nerea imagines Lewis' mouth full of toothpaste foam, saying 'bless you.' His mouth full of foam, as it was the day she met him in a pub in Oxford.

12

'You're the thief?' Dolores said out loud, surprised, to her sister Luisa, when she saw her taking a flower from the vase on the bar in the restaurant. Dolores did not know that Bittori was so near, and heard everything. If she had known, she would not have spoken so loudly. She would not have betrayed her sister.

Bittori punished Luisa for stealing flowers. For a month she would not be allowed to go out to run errands. Bittori knew what Luisa liked best. And while Luisa was in the kitchen, she was not to read the cheap romantic novels she hid under her apron. Bittori made her write out recipes. All of the recipes of all the dishes they made in the restaurant. Three tablespoons of sugar, two of flour... Bittori had Luisa writing out recipes on the kitchen table for nearly a whole month. Sea bream in sauce, tuna in tomato sauce... While Bittori dictated the recipes to her, she watched her out of the corner of her eye and sighed, wondering what they should do with this girl. Always lost in her own world, the girl had been contaminated by those second-rate books she read. Crème caramel, walnut cream, rice pudding... While Luisa was writing out recipes she had only one worry on her mind: while Herman was out fishing this time, he would not find the flowers in the sea that would bring him luck. With this thought tormenting her and a whole month without going to the seashore, Luisa started to look like a wilted flower.

13

Which photo to show her mother? Which photo to start with? With her mind on these questions, she went into her mother's room and was startled to find her there awake. There she was with her eyes wide open and all alone in the room. There was no one in the other bed. They must have sent Pilar for a test, she thinks. It seems strange to her to see the room without the two women in it. Something else occurs to her. Something is missing. The sound of bagpipes. And words. The downpour of words. She wonders where all the words that Pili has said have gone. Perhaps they escaped through the window, or are still stuck to the walls in the room, waiting to jump out again.

When she goes in, she approaches her mother uncomfortably. Her mother's direct gaze, the silence in the room. To break the uncomfortable silence, she says 'Mum.' Mum. And her mother repeats the word: 'Mum.'

Taking advantage of the fact that her mother is awake, Nerea quickly takes the photos out of her purse. She looks at the one taken on the beach, and smiles. She sees herself at the water's edge, seven or eight years old, sitting inside a wall of sand. And, as happened the last time she saw the photo, it seems to her that she can smell the sun cream her mother used to put on her. Then she picks up the photo taken in the kitchen at the Izagirre Restaurant, the one with the six women looking up. She holds it out toward her mother's hands and her mother takes it. Luisa holds onto the photo the way a newborn holds onto an offered hand. Almost with inertia. The way Maialen first held her hand when she was a newborn.

'Look at all the people here, Mum. Look down here, who's this young woman,' she says. It seems like no one is listening and she speaks to her mother louder than other times.

Nerea's mother looks at the photo, and at the same time, Nerea looks at her. It's hard for her to believe that the young girl in the photo is the woman before her now. One of them, the one in the photo, is a green leaf. The other a dry leaf carried downstream in the current. A fallen leaf carried by the river. But, as if the water of the creek had refreshed the dry leaf, suddenly something revives Luisa and, looking at the photo, she mentions some names. Simply hearing those names gives Nerea a lump in her throat and her eyes fill with tears. Thank goodness they're alone, she thinks, as she dries her tears on the sleeve of her shirt.

'Mum,' Nerea says urgently. She wants her mother to look at her, because she wants to hear her own name in her mother's voice. But, as if her voice had entered her mother's world violently, Luisa's face changes suddenly. The smile she had shown when she recognised the women in the photo disappears and she is expressionless again. She looks at Nerea, but not in the eye, rather at her forehead, and then fixes her eyes on the white wall across from her. She is lost again. The taut string of the helium balloon has again slipped through Nerea's fingers.

Nerea rests her forehead against her mother's headboard. Her heart is pounding. She raises her eyes and sees the photograph taken in the Izagirre Restaurant on the sheet, fallen from her mother's hands. She picks it up and puts it in her appointment book. There is a colour photograph among the other pictures. One of the ones with that artificial colour of early colour photographs. Her mother ironing clothes in the kitchen at home, and at her side are Xabier and Nerea. She must be six and Xabier about eight. Her mother has her hand up, as if to beg her father not to take the picture. Nerea thinks it must be the first photograph her father took after buying the colour camera. He would have wanted to try it out at home, and her mother wouldn't have wanted to be in it in her house clothes and unprepared.

Nerea spent hours watching how her mother ironed clothes, chin on the old cloth she would put down on the table. While her mother ironed, she would often have a piece of paper on the part of the table the cloth didn't cover, and she would draw there, close to the warmth of the iron. *Whoosh-whoosh*, she hears. It's the strokes of the iron that she used to hear as she drew. And she breathes in deep, inhaling the smell of clean clothes, the smell of the family. And she keeps on drawing her picture, the usual picture: a mountain, with the sun coming out from behind it, two fat clouds nearby, and right in the middle, a farmhouse with a red roof. Once her mother yelled at Xabier for playing with his toy cowboys in his room, telling him not to make noise because the neighbours would come up. Xabier was making the plastic cowboys commit suicide by jumping off the bed. But he was jumping with them too, and making a lot of noise. Her mother had the radio on, as Bittori used to in the restaurant, and while the little girl draws, she listens to the news, the lottery numbers, Elena Francis, a novel...

She sees her mother's hands scooping up a warm little

mountain of ironed clothes and over the top of the pile her mother says 'take these to your room.' And she sees a young girl going down the chilly hall with her chin buried in those warm clothes, breathing in the smell of the clean washing, the smell of family.

Until the nurse enters the room, she doesn't realise that she is resting her chin on the sheet with the word *hospital* written on it. The nurse asks her to leave so she can clean up the room. Nerea gathers up the photos she had on her lap, and when she stands up, her mother's hand grasps her arm. She is startled and asks the nurse to wait a minute.

'What is it, Mum?' she asks.

'When are we going?'

'Where?'

She asks her where, but she already has an idea what her mother will say.

'To the lighthouse.'

Nerea doesn't know how to answer. The nurse tells her she hasn't got all day and she'll have to leave the room.

She leans against the wall in the hallway and holds her head with one hand. She has a headache. She could cry again but the hospital corridor is so white and so cold that no tears come out.

Two nurses go past her, one of them pushing an empty wheelchair. One says something to the other about three dead, shrugging her shoulders. The other one shakes her head and sighs. Nerea guesses that they're talking about the explosion the previous day and this makes her want to cry even more.

'You can go in.' She hears a voice from behind her. They've finished cleaning.

She would like to go in saying 'here I am, Mum,' but she's afraid to break the silence of the room and she dares only to cough. She coughs. Three times. Her mother notices that she's there again.

'Do you see the ocean?' her mother says, looking at the wall across from her.

'Yes, Mum,' Nerea answers, and she thinks she should ask the nurses for the wheelchair. It would do her mother good to get out of the room. Spending so many hours in the same room is giving her hallucinations. It would be no bad thing for her to be able to at least spend Christmas at home, where, instead of smelling purées and medicines, she can take in the smell of family.

14

Last night it felt like something was missing at home. Lewis was out and, since she is used to finding him there when she comes home, she felt like she had wandered into a strange house. She smelled his absence even though she knew he wouldn't be home in time for dinner because he was having dinner with the people from his Basque class. Ever since he came to the Basque Country to live, he rarely goes out at night without her. He went out with Maite and Iñaki a few times when she was pregnant, but otherwise he never goes out at night without her.

Lewis is enjoying the Basque language school. He has made a lot of friends. He needed something like that too, thinks Nerea, he was suffocating at home. But she still felt uncomfortable tonight, uneasy, like when she's in bed and suddenly thinks she's left the tap on in the bathroom sink. Until she gets up to see that no water is coming out, she won't be able to relax. She knew she wouldn't relax until Lewis came home. And Lewis comes home really late, the smell of alcohol on his breath. He trips over the rug before lying down on the bed. Even though she is awake, Nerea doesn't open an eye.

In the morning, she leaves her husband asleep in bed. On

the way to work, she turns on the car radio without thinking, automatically, but immediately thinks the better of it and turns it off. It's all about the previous day's explosion. Ever since Karlos left the Basque Country, she can't listen to such news. Can't bear it. She takes it as a deeply personal thing. As if the explosion had penetrated her very guts.

She arrives at the office and sees Fidel first of all. This is the perfect opportunity to challenge him about the headline, but she no longer feels like it, her anger has drained away. Now she thinks it's better to just let it go. She is working on a report about wind power. She has to make a number of phone calls and, on top of that, Fidel has left an announcement about a press conference today on her desk. Her stomach starts churning again. And her head. She has to be at the press conference in an hour. She doesn't have time to start anything. She hears a sort of humming. She feels dizzy. She sees her pack of cigarettes on the desk and realises she must be in a very bad way indeed since she doesn't feel like smoking at all.

She picks up the newspaper next to the cigarette pack, thinking that holding onto it will help with the dizziness. On the front page is a photo of a car in pieces, and a number leaps out at her: three. Three dead. She remembers the hospital nurses shrugging and wonders how that figure makes the person who blew up the car feel. Will he take that number with indifference or will it play over and over in his mind, three, three, three, as if it were a drum? Or when he hears the number three, does he see the faces of three friends dead or tortured or arrested or beaten, and do these images stop him from feeling any repentance or compassion? Or even if he sees the images of his friends, will he keep hearing the drum? Three, three, three.

She turns over the newspaper, as if by placing the photo face down on the desk she could make reality disappear. Because what is not seen does not exist. This is what journalism has taught her. On the other side of the newspaper there is a photo of a smiling family, as if the two sides of the newspaper were the two sides of a coin. It is a family from Murcia and they're holding the cheque they won in a television competition, all of them smiling. The two sides of the lottery. The father is holding onto his son's arm and raising it high in a gesture of victory. And Nerea is envious. Not because of the money they won, but because they have nothing to do with the car in pieces in the photo on the other side of the newspaper. She has nothing to do with it either, but she feels the burden of it. She wants to be like the family from Murcia and not live in fear of what the newspaper will print the next day. How peaceful to be born in Murcia, she thinks. Or in Oxford.

She needs to talk to someone and calls Maite.

'How are you, Nere?' Maite answers the phone.

'Fine.'

'And your mother?'

'Well, all right. She's started remembering a few things. Some names...'

'That's good.' Maite falls silent. She is waiting to hear the reason for the call. But on the other end of the line, Nerea has fallen silent too. She can't get the words out.

'And Lewis and your daughter?' asks Maite, just to say something.

'Yesterday was horrible, wasn't it?' says Nerea, without hearing the question. The topic makes her feel raw inside and she needs to bring it out into the open.

Maite understands Nerea's worry, she knows that with the

news of Karlos' return, this topic has made her more nervous than at other times.

'The editorial office must be going crazy with all this,' she says.

'Well, yes, you can imagine.'

They speak as if about something inevitable, as if what happened were a natural phenomenon, like an earthquake, for example. They speak the same way when something like that happens. As if it were something that had always existed. And it is like that, because for both Nerea and Maite it has always existed. Those of her generation know no other reality.

'And how are you? Do you need any help?'

'It's okay. This too shall pass.' Nerea's voice trembles.

'Are you okay?'

No. She is not okay. Like a car bomb, something has exploded in her mind. When she stops, everything comes crashing down on top of her. Her world is full of cracks suddenly. And water is leaking out through the cracks here and there.

'Are you okay?' Maite asks again.

She can't answer. It's like a huge cloak has been thrown over her and she is in its shade, everything has gone dark for her. She doesn't see the computer before her. She sees images that appear and disappear before her eyes: Maialen calling from her bed, Lewis coming to bed half drunk from the dinner with his Basque class, her mother's hands holding onto the old photograph, Fidel, the car in pieces, Karlos.

'Do you know anything else about Karlos?'

She didn't mean to ask this question; it just slipped out.

'Not much. I'll ask Iñaki if you want, he'll know more...' answers Maite.

'Don't bother Iñaki,' she interrupts, 'Don't ask him anything.'

She's still dizzy. She puts her hand to her forehead.

'When are you going to the hospital?'

'I don't know, when I can, at noon.'

'Shall we meet there?'

'At three?'

'Okay. And we'll have lunch there.'

When she hangs up the phone, she sees herself from above, as if she were a bird that had flown into the office. She sees a woman at her desk in the editorial office. Her elbows are on the desk and her head is in her hands. She has her eyes closed. She looks exhausted, and then she realises that she's like her father driving on a coast road full of curves, going endlessly from one curve to the next and each time saying 'another one down!' Drops of sweat fall from her forehead. And, like her father, she sees herself telling everyone around her, 'don't worry, I know how to drive.' But the last curve goes up a hill. And the car doesn't have enough power to get up the hill. She will have to ask for help. This time she'll have to.

15

As Herman was trying to reach the life preserver that was dancing on the water, everything went black.

'You had a good fight with the ocean, boy,' said the captain when Herman woke up on a bed in a room on a ship.

He raised his body and sat up on the bed, afraid. Eyes wide open.

'Easy, boy, easy. You won that fight.'

When he left the room, the captain warned the others on the boat. The poor boy still had his head full of ocean. And the fishermen kept on doing what they were doing, as if they hadn't heard anything, gazing distrustfully at the ocean before them. Trying to guess who had really won that fight.

16

Maite has often heard Nerea's stories about her relatives, but until today she had not met Aunt Dolores. They asked for the fixed menu at the hospital cafeteria and now they're sitting around a table, all three of them, Dolores, Maite, and Nerea, with their trays. Nerea calmed down a bit on her way to the hospital, but her nerves are tight. She feels the calm that comes after a good cry, however it's not a peaceful calm, but a truce offered in the calm that comes after pain, a rest to catch your breath. She is not okay, but she doesn't want her aunt to see her with a long face, so she's making an effort. Even so, she feels like she has a long face every time one of them looks at her. Especially when Maite looks at her. After their telephone conversation, Maite has been worried about her, and she can't hide it no matter what she does. Dolores is also worried because Luisa seems to have gone downhill a bit more, but she doesn't want to show her distress and all three paste big smiles on their faces while Dolores tells about what Nerea was like as a child.

'It's not surprising that she became a journalist in the end. She always wanted to know everything. You know,' she says to Maite, 'every time we came from Germany, she had to go through everything I was carrying in my old suitcase, as if she had to find something in there, a treasure. I'd say she was more pleased to see my suitcase than to see me.'

'That can't be true,' says Maite.

'You know what the treasure was, right? A present,' responds Nerea, and all three laugh.

'You two were together in England, right?' Nerea's aunt asks.

They both answer with a nod, Maite with her mouth full and Nerea as she pushes her peas from one side of the plate to the other with her fork.

Dolores tells them that she knew about Maite because Luisa had told her in the letters she sent to Germany that Nerea had gone to Oxford with a friend.

'"Thank God she's there with a Basque person," your mother used to say, "the winters in England are so sad." That's just what your mother used to say, that winters in England are very sad, even though she had never been to England herself. She must have seen it in a film, or in one of those romantic novels she liked so much, who knows. Nerea, your mother often mentioned you in her letters. She was worried about you. Just like she was worried about Paolo since he was ill by then' – her eyes get red and after a moment, she sighs. 'Well, with this menu, who wants to go to the Arzak restaurant? It is Arzak, isn't it?'

'Yes, Arzak. One day we'll go there, Aunt Dolores.'

'Yes, one day... You can pay for my meal with the treasure you found in my suitcase!'

The three of them laugh again.

'Aunt Dolores, first I thought we could ask the doctor's permission to take Mum home with us at Christmas,' says Nerea. 'At least for Christmas Eve. I'd like all of us to be able to celebrate together that evening, like we used to. Do you think the doctor will let us take her home if we ask, even if it's just for one day?'

'I don't know,' her aunt answers. 'If it's just for one day, maybe… We'll have to ask him.'

'Well, I have to go back to the office,' says Nerea then, but as soon as she says it, Pili runs into the cafeteria, out of breath.

She says that Luisa is talking non-stop and they need to come up to the room quickly, please, come up, she seems to be very nervous. And she runs off again. Dolores and Nerea go after her and Maite just stands there. Then Nerea looks back and gestures to Maite that she should come too. Now all four of them are in the elevator.

Luisa is talking and talking, Pili explains in the elevator, but she doesn't understand anything because she's talking in Basque. She seems to be very nervous.

They run down the hallway but when they get to the room, they stop for a second.

'You first,' Nerea says to her aunt.

'No, you go ahead,' her aunt answers. And she almost shoves her toward the door.

Nerea goes in first, with the other three women behind her.

Luisa is sitting on the bed craning her neck with her eyes open wide.

'Mum,' says Nerea.

But her mother doesn't look at her. She is staring at Aunt Dolores behind her. You could hear a pin drop. They are all as quiet as can be.

'Come here,' Luisa orders Dolores in a tone of voice that Nerea finds strange. When Dolores goes over to her, Luisa pulls her closer by the neck. Dolores swallows hard. Luisa grabs the collar of Dolores' shirt in her hand and says 'let's go,' looking her right in the eye.

Dolores barely dares to ask the question.

'Go where?'

And Luisa brings her mouth close to her sister's ear. She says something under her breath and Nerea guesses what it is. She guesses that she asked to go to the lighthouse.

For a second Dolores' eyes fill with tears. Her eyes widen and she doesn't take her gaze off of Luisa. She is swallowing hard again, looking questioningly at her sister. Luisa has not yet let go of the collar of her shirt. Dolores tugs herself loose and runs out of the room.

It frightens Nerea that her aunt left the room like that. Until today she had never seen Dolores lose control. When she heard what Luisa said, her face changed as if she were seeing a ghost from the past, and she left the room wounded. In tears.

Nerea goes over to her mother and takes her hands. They are shaking. She tells Maite to please call the doctor and tell him her mother is having a nervous breakdown.

Little by little, Luisa seems to be calming down.

'Take it easy, Mum, easy does it,' says Nerea, without letting go of her hands.

And she stays like that until her mother's breathing calms. When the doctor arrives, he asks them to leave the room because he wants to be alone with Luisa. When they go out, they find Dolores in the hallway, facing the wall and leaning against it, taking deep breaths with her head resting on her arms.

'Aunt Dolores, are you okay?'

'Yes, yes. Go to work and don't worry. I'll stay here.'

Nerea sees her aunt fleeing. She doesn't want to look Nerea in the eye. Nerea can't see her sparkling eyes.

'Will you call me after you've seen the doctor?' Nerea asks her aunt.

'Yes, don't worry, I'll call you.'

'But are you okay?'

'Yes, I am. I need to go to the restroom.'

Dolores disappears down the hallway and Maite and Nerea are left alone.

'Shall I take you to the office?' Maite asks.

'No, that's okay, I have the car.'

They reach the parking lot and as soon as Nerea says, 'I'm here,' she starts crying, sobbing. The tears flood out. Maite puts an arm around her shoulders.

'Take it easy, Nere.'

'Sorry, Maite, it's just that...'

'Take it easy, have a good cry.'

'I can't take it anymore. I don't even know who to talk to anymore.' She hears a drumbeat inside her. Hundreds of mustachioed men playing the drums.

'I'm right here.'

'Thank goodness for you... I tell Lewis I'm fed up and, okay, he understands, but I don't know if he really gets how fed up I am. A while ago I started telling him I got mad at Fidel at work, and I've just had enough and I don't have time for anything, and I'm so worried about my mother... And he said yes, he understood, but then added, with his English elegance, that at least I get some fresh air, but he spends the whole day at home without going out and without seeing anyone, and that's also very hard. He didn't say it like that, but that's what he meant. And I ended up consoling him. Do you understand me, Maite? And who's going to console me? Who?'

'Take it easy.'

'Lately Lewis has been wanting to get out of the house. He's excited because he's made friends in his Basque class and I understand but… The other day he came back from dinner late and drunk.'

'You're not jealous of him, are you? You brought him from England, but other people get to know him too, right?'

'That's not it, Maite, that's not it. It's everything all together. I can't take it anymore. I don't feel like going to work. Then I'm tired at work before I even start. And I spend the whole day there. The time I don't spend at the hospital, I spend there. I hardly even see my daughter. I know how she sleeps by heart. I don't know, I've been at a loss ever since this stuff started with my mother. I was very busy before too, but it was different, now something has *cracked* inside me and on top of everything else I'm more sensitive than ever. And the worst of it is that it's all been too much for my aunt, who has always been so strong until now, and that's really all we needed. I just keep going over it and over it in my mind, Maite. Sometimes I think I've done everything wrong.'

'Wrong? Do you really mean that Maialen is the result of something you did wrong? Iñaki and I would love to have such luck. Don't you realise how lucky you are, Nere?'

Nerea's telephone rings and her face changes. As does her voice.

'Hello? Yes, speaking.' She dries her tears on her arm. It's the expert she had contacted for her report on wind power.

She holds the telephone with one hand while she goes through her purse with the other, looking for her notebook and pen.

'Yes, yes. I'll call you in an hour then. It will be five or six questions. Yes, we hope to publish it next week. Yes, we'll send a photographer. What's the address?'

She rests her notebook on the hood of the car and writes the address in it. She lifts up one leg to stop her purse from falling to the ground, and she can't move a muscle if she doesn't want the telephone, the notebook, the pen and all to fall to the ground. Maite is looking at her, thinking that her friend looks like a Chinese juggler, doing amazing things to keep the plates from falling. 'Now that's balance,' she says, looking at Nerea. 'That's balance.'

17

Luisa found Herman's gaze strange. After waiting for him for three weeks, she almost didn't recognise the ashen boy with the bowed head who stepped off the Urkiolamendi. When he saw her at the port, he said 'Luisa' in a trembling voice and Luisa noticed his frightened eyes. Some other fishermen helped Herman from the ship as if he were ill, and it was not long until Luisa realised that Herman really was ill, for his mind was full of towering waves.

She felt a wave slap her cheek when she saw him, and felt the inescapable weight of guilt. She wanted to tell Herman she tried to throw the flowers that would bring him luck into the water, but she couldn't, she was grounded. But she said nothing. She had seen his lost gaze, and understood that he wouldn't understand anything. So she ran home to seek consolation in one of her hidden novels.

18

Blank pages, faxes, photocopies, loose newspaper pages. In the afternoons the papers in the editorial office take on a life of their own and fall from above like snowflakes. They might land on an ashtray full of cigarettes, or on a plastic drinking glass, or on the forgotten photo of a politician.

Nerea hears telephones, faxes, parts of conversations. The plastic glass on her desk has traces of dried coffee in it. To warm and calm her belly, which is empty except for cigarette smoke, she gets a coffee from the machine. The coffee machine doesn't give her any change again today. Someone should call the repair man, but since no one is responsible for that and everyone is up to their ears in work, no one does it. After two sips of her coffee, she feels like smoking again. Often she drinks coffee just in order to feel like smoking, even though she knows that she'll have heartburn later.

Without lifting his eyes from his screen, Santi, who sits next to her, says, 'A three-by-two ad is going on your page.'

'I have to have the ads again?' answers Nerea without taking the cigarette from her lips.

'Fidel saaaaaaid,' he says, putting his hands together as if in prayer, and looking toward the heavens.

'And what am I supposed to say now? Ameeeeeeen?' answers Nerea. She takes the cigarette from her lips and sets it on the edge of the ashtray. It looks like a little chimney there.

Fidel's decisions are driving her up the wall. She has to shorten a report she had ready due to last-minute changes. She has often protested because they put last-minute advertising on her page, but today she won't go over to Fidel to complain. She doesn't even want to see him. She doesn't want so much as a whiff of his revolting aftershave. She doesn't even care what her report looks like. She just wants to finish up and go home as soon as possible. That's all. Finish and run. She picks up the cigarette again from the ashtray, but it's down to the butt and she stubs it out.

Lately, she's been running like the White Rabbit in *Alice in Wonderland*, she thinks, running from one place to another with her watch in her hand. Running and in a hurry. But she's already fallen down a hole, just like Alice, and now that she's started falling, she doesn't care. On her way down she sees various images: her mother in the hospital calling for Herman, Karlos at a bus station with a big bag, Lewis bursting out laughing at the dinner with his Basque class, Maialen calling from her bed, her aunt in tears... She feels, like Alice, that she has tumbled into a strange world and she's looking for a way to get out of that world but, unlike Alice, she doesn't have the opportunity to choose from among lots of doors. She sees only a single door before her. The one that shows the way forward.

'Nerea, have you gone deaf? Telephone,' says Santi, without lifting his gaze from his screen.

It's Maite. She asks if everything is okay. She's been worried ever since the hospital this morning. Nerea answers that she's fine, looking at the plastic glass in front of her. A little flustered, but okay.

'And is your aunt okay?'

Nerea tells her that her aunt's reaction worries her. Dolores hasn't slowed down for a minute since she arrived. After spending the whole day at the hospital, she goes home and doesn't stop there either. For a moment Nerea wonders how she would manage without her aunt's help and, to shoo the image from her mind as fast as possible, she shakes her head hard from one side to the other as if she were trying to shake off a fly that had landed on her face.

'Iñaki was with Karlos at noon.'

Maite has recovered her ability to speak plainly.

'Where?' asks Nerea quickly. She feels a warmth in her belly, as if she had taken a sip of wine.

'In the Old Town. Iñaki said he looks good. Older, but pretty good.

Nerea falls silent. Her gut is boiling.

'Well, the thing is, he asked about you. If we still see each other, what you've been up to. If you still hang out in the Old Town. Questions.'

Nerea feels like she's under attack. As if a hooded figure were attacking her with a knife. She imagines a ghost mentioning her name. *And what can you tell me about Nerea?* It would have been better if she had not known that Karlos was in town and had mentioned her name. She feels like someone is following her, the way Karlos had the police following him for so many years. And she feels like she's suffocating. Even the spit in her throat has dried up.

'Karlos told him that for the moment he can be here. At least for the moment. But he can't relax either. And they talked about the situation, but without getting into deep water. He has lots to tell him, and they're going to get together again the day after tomorrow.'

'What did he say about me?'

'Karlos?'

'No, Iñaki.'

'I don't know, I didn't ask.'

'He wouldn't have told him where I live and all?'

'I don't know, Nere. I'll find out. I don't think so.'

She asks Maite to please not tell Karlos anything about her life, and says she's very busy with work and needs to get back to it. She doesn't want to hear anything more. She feels dizzy. Her head is about to explode. Karlos is thinking of staying in town. But why does he have to stay here, she thinks. Why here? Why does he have to ask after her? Given that he gave no explanations when he left, why is he coming around now demanding explanations? She doesn't want to see him. She doesn't want to see how he has aged, doesn't want to see Lazarus rising. 'Stay in your tomb, Lazarus,' she says under her breath.

Right after she hangs up the phone, it rings again. The phone is still warm. It's her brother. He's at the hospital with Dolores. They've spoken with the doctor and, even though he said the nervous episode that their mother had after lunch is normal, Xabier thought the doctor looked nervous, and when Dolores mentioned the idea of taking their mother home for Christmas Eve, he answered with a resounding no. It could be really risky to take their mother out as she's in a very delicate state, and the best thing would be for her to stay at the hospital, just in case.

'Do you know what's going on with Aunt Dolores?' he asks. 'She's very upset.'

Nerea puts her hand to her forehead. She doesn't know

anything either but it's normal, she's very worried about her sister's state, and it must be very upsetting. And now Nerea realises that lately she has spoken to Xabier only on the telephone, so to wrap up the conversation, she says 'When are we going to get together then, eh, brother?' She hasn't called him *brother* for a long time, the way she used to when she was young. When she started studying English she started calling him *brother* and has said it many times since then. But not in recent years. They haven't talked much, they're both always busy with work, and when that word pops out, it seems to her that she sees a ray of light. A breath of fresh air wafting into the suffocating atmosphere of the editorial office.

She hangs up the phone and closes her eyes. And then a drawing from the story Lewis reads to Maialen every night comes to her. Alice has gone over to a small door and is looking at the flower garden on the other side.

'Was that ad three-by-two or two-by-three?' she asks Santi who sits next to her, and she looks over the text from top to bottom, without being able to decide what to cut. She should tell Fidel it's fine as it is, and why does he have to put last-minute ads on her page. But she won't say anything to him. She doesn't want the smell of the flower garden from *Alice in Wonderland* to mix with the smell of his aftershave. She lights a cigarette and sets it down on the ashtray. The chimney starts smoking again.

19

Nerea opens the door at home and smells soup. Not the kind from a packet. It was prepared from the broth that Dolores made. She used to smell a similar smell when she came home from school as a child and went into the kitchen. She would leave her books in the living room and find her mother there in the kitchen under the fluorescent light, drying her hands on a dishcloth, waiting for her father to come home from work. Her hands smelled of garlic as she cupped Nerea's chin and asked what she did at school. The house smells of that long-ago smell and she breathes in deeply after closing the door.

She goes into the house with the same sensation she used to have when she first started working at the newspaper as a young woman and would set off eagerly and curiously in search of news, believing that she would find information. Information she was lacking. She needs information about her mother, about what happened at the hospital this morning. She doesn't understand why her aunt reacted like that. Why she couldn't stop crying. Dolores will have to tell her what the lighthouse is about.

The door to Maialen's room is closed. She must be asleep.

Nerea finds Lewis in the study. He is reading various pages he has under the table lamp, with his glasses on the end of his nose. When he sees Nerea at the door, he raises a hand as if to ask her to wait until he finishes reading the last paragraph. Nerea raises her arm and makes circles in the air with her finger to say they'll talk later, and goes to the kitchen.

There is her aunt. Standing by the kettle. She is drying her hands on her apron. But she doesn't cup Nerea's chin in her hands to ask how school was, like her mother used to. She says 'How was work?' as if from far away, without looking her in the eye. Dolores is ashamed of what happened at the hospital. Today was the first time she ever cried in front of Nerea.

'How are you?' Nerea asks, worried because the woman in front of her looks like a stranger. She needs some of Tinker Bell's gold fairy dust.

'Fine. I made you some soup, it'll do you good.'

'Yes, but are you okay, Aunt Dolores?'

'Yes, I'm okay.'

'And how's Mum?' she asks, seeing that her aunt doesn't want to talk about herself.

'She talked a lot today. She said some meaningless things and others with too much meaning... I don't know, sometimes it looks like she's coming back to reality, but then suddenly her head goes flying off somewhere again and she starts repeating anything she hears.'

Dolores doesn't stop doing things while she says all this. She puts the plates on the table, stirs the soup, fills a pitcher of water. She doesn't look Nerea in the eye for even one second. Nerea wonders, when her mother says she wants to go to the lighthouse, whether her aunt thinks that's a meaningful thing or a meaningless one. Given Dolores' reaction, Nerea thinks it must have a bit of meaning to it.

'Xabier told me the doctor said he won't give us permission to bring Mum home on Christmas Eve.'

'Yes, he said it's better to have her where she has a doctor nearby, just in case.'

Lewis appears. He gives her a kiss and fills a glass with water from the tap. Then he puts an effervescent aspirin in the glass. He takes the glass and a banana and goes back to the study. He mumbles that he has a deadline coming up for work. Nerea hears *deadline* or something like it and he's gone. She doesn't understand anything, not because he said it in English, but because she's thinking about something else: her husband isn't over his hangover yet. The one from his dinner.

When she tries the soup, images from her childhood return to her mind. She sees her mother serving soup to her father, and she can barely see her father's face behind the steam rising from the soup. She can't remember her father's face. That's a first. Then, the question she's been holding in all day comes out.

'Aunt Dolores, why does Mum keep saying she wants to go to the lighthouse? She told me the same thing earlier. Does it mean anything?'

Her aunt is doing the washing up, scrubbing the kettle. She doesn't turn when she hears the question.

'Just things from her youth that have somehow stuck with her. It's nothing.'

It's clear that she does not want to continue this conversation. They both fall silent. The water from the tap can be heard falling on the kettle, nothing else, and occasionally Dolores coughs. Looking at her back, it seems to Nerea that a layer of paint is flaking off of Dolores' wardrobe too. However, it isn't enough yet for the colour underneath to show. And as she asks the next question, she feels like an investigative reporter. One of the ones that challenges everything.

'But why did you react like that? If it really were nothing?'

Dolores dries her hands on the dishcloth and sits down across from Nerea. She throws the dishcloth down on the table, hard, as if giving up. She sighs and starts talking, looking at the table. She still doesn't look Nerea in the eye.

'You don't know how much she loved going to the lighthouse and looking out at the sea from there. She always made the excuse that she was running errands in order to escape to the lighthouse on an old bicycle we had at the restaurant. We often went together. She looked straight at the sea, in a way that she was unable to do with people, and she breathed in deeply. It looked like she was saying 'Here I am' to the sea. Here I am, ready to face even the biggest wave. And she asked me to do the same thing. And she asked me if I could smell the salt, if I could feel the crash of the waves against the rocks on the bottoms of my feet, if I could hear the gush of the water after the waves broke...' She takes another breath, as if she were thinking about whether to tell more or not. 'After she had spent an entire month without going down to the sea, she looked like a wilted flower, she needed fresh air. Bittori grounded her for a month, a month without going out to run errands, a month of sitting in the kitchen writing out recipes. And there she sat, without being able to go to the lighthouse. But even after her punishment, she didn't return to the lighthouse. She suddenly stopped going. I asked her many times why she wouldn't return to the lighthouse and she said that she was angry with the sea. That the sea had stolen Herman from her. I heard that more than once. There was a fisherman named Herman around at that time, and all of a sudden he stopped going to sea too. Suddenly. As if he too were angry with the sea. And I don't know what happened between them after that, but I do remember that your mother didn't want to see Herman any more. I would hear her crying every night in the bed next to mine, and sometimes she mentioned Herman's name in her sleep. Not the way a lover's name is mentioned, but angrily, cursing him'.

While her aunt is talking, Nerea keeps very still. Dolores could stop telling the story at any avoidable movement, word or glance. Nerea is almost holding her breath, focused on what her aunt is saying.

'Your mother was devastated then, and I don't know if I did enough to help her. I was just starting to see Sebastian then and I didn't have enough time... After so many years... She hardly even remembers her own name and she has to remember all this...'

Even though it was hard for her to start talking, now that she's started, Dolores doesn't stop. Even though Nerea is dropping with exhaustion, she keeps her eyes on Dolores. It is only when Lewis comes into the kitchen again that the two women realise the clock on the wall says it's midnight. Dolores has been talking for nearly two hours. She talked non-stop about Nerea's mother. Telling a story about her mother that until now Nerea hadn't known. Dolores was like a bottle of champagne. It's often difficult to get the cork out, it has to be forced but, once the bottle is open, there's no stopping the rush of bubbles.

20

Herman told her he wouldn't be going out in the next fishing season. He needed a break. And Luisa understood. But the next time, he came up with another excuse, and yet another one the time after that. In the fourth season, he told her he was ready to go to sea, and he told the captain of the Urkiolamendi as well, but he didn't show up at the port in the morning. Those who went to his house to look for him found him lying on the bed reeking of alcohol. With his street clothes still on.

He stayed on dry land during the next fishing season too. Unable to overcome the fear of the ocean that had taken hold of him. While Luisa worked at the restaurant, Herman wandered around here and there. From one bar to the next.

One day, when they were at the lighthouse, Luisa told him that she couldn't go on like that. He had to do something. Herman's eyes flared the way a sea that looks calm can suddenly flare up, and he shouted at her to leave him in peace. Luisa smelled the alcohol in the words that came out of his mouth and suddenly it felt like a stranger was talking to her. She tried to calm him down, but that made things worse. He pushed her hands off of him violently, and by the time he raised his arm to the level of his ear, Luisa knew that the sea had stolen her Herman. That was not Herman; the boy she had known had stayed among the waves. The owner of the hand she felt on her cheek couldn't be the same boy she had met at a dance in the town square, the one who had held her so tenderly around the waist. It couldn't be the same one, even though both of them had hands roughened by the sea.

21

When Karlos left town, Nerea spent hours in her bedroom with the door closed, lying on her bed with a pillow over her head. Or staring out of the window without seeing anything. Her mother stood outside her room, asking her to open the door, to please open the door. And she said no, to let her be, to leave her in peace. The pain she felt was so great that no one else could imagine it, that's what she thought, least of all her mother. How then could she open the door? Almost twenty years later she learned from her aunt that her mother did know something about the pain that love can bring. Nerea closed the door on her mother then and now she doesn't know what to do in order to be able to open that door again.

It hurts to look at the photo in front of her. As when she sucks on a lemon, her eyes narrow with the sting she feels when looking at her mother's image. It is a photo taken by her father on the day she left for Oxford. She and her mother are at the airport. Even though she is smiling, Luisa's brow is furrowed, and her eyes look deeper than possible. Her eyes do not agree with her smile. Until today, Nerea hadn't seen the sadness and worry in those eyes; before today she had never looked carefully at the image of her mother in this photo.

Aunt Dolores told her that in the letters her mother sent to Germany she always mentioned how much she missed Nerea ever since she had gone to Oxford. She says that her mother sounds worried in those letters. Her mother was worried about what had happened with Karlos. And now, looking at the photograph, she sees the worry her aunt mentioned in her mother's eyes. There is a smile on her lips but her eyes are sad.

Nerea was abroad for a full year and her mother decided not to say anything about her father's illness until she returned. Her mother also withstood this alone. In her letters to Aunt Dolores in Germany, she explained that she didn't want to worry her children so she kept the news about their father from them. Just as she now tries to hide the word *hospital* on the sheets.

As Nerea looks at the photograph, she remembers how many times she forgot to call her mother from Oxford and how little she wrote her. She sees her mother in the kitchen at home ironing the clothes. *Thrum-thrum*. But there is no little girl drawing pictures on the table. There is no brother in the background, jumping on the bed as his toy cowboys commit suicide. Only the radio is heard, echoing on the kitchen walls. And a deep sigh from her mother, as she tries to iron the collar of her father's shirt.

Nerea would dearly love to turn back the time machine and call her mother from Oxford, and tell her everything is going very well and she misses her, and ask how she's doing. But, being unable to turn back time, she has to say those words to her mother now. Now she would like to ask her how she's doing, and tell her she misses her, but she fears that she has missed her chance. She has arrived too late. The things that are not said earlier cannot always be said later, and one cannot give after death the hugs that were left ungiven in life.

But her mother is not yet in the grave, and Nerea still has a tiny bit of hope. A small ray of light. She wants to offer something to her mother and she believes that her mother is still able to perceive that offering.

She has to go quickly or she'll miss her flight. A hug and she tells her mother to stop giving her advice for once, the aeroplane is about to leave, and she's about to miss it. Maite is waiting for her on the other side of passport control. It feels like she's spent her whole life running. She doesn't experience things as they happen; it's only when she sees a photograph that she fully appreciates an experience. She is afraid that one day she'll stop to remember all the moments she missed along the way and the world will simply leap over her and go ahead without her.

And once again, she would like to turn the clock back now, the way a video can be rewound, and stop, wrapped up in one of her mother's hugs. Even though her name comes on the loudspeakers to ask her to please get on the plane, she would like to stay there, bound to her mother. Let all the aeroplanes in the world fly. Let them go all the way around the world while she stays in her mother's embrace. She now feels that she missed an aeroplane that day.

It is difficult to see herself in the photograph. She wants to get away from her mother as fast as possible, wants her to take away the hand she has around her waist so she can run for the plane. She is not looking at the camera, nor at her father behind the camera. She is looking farther on, toward passport control. Maite is waiting for her there. And she is eager to get there. To get there and get away, as fast as possible, from the surroundings that are smothering her.

22

Ever since she was little she knew that her aunt's old leather suitcase must hold a treasure. She always knew it and, slowly, very slowly, she has begun to find the treasure, one that has travelled great distances over the years, the treasure of the past.

At home, Nerea notices that her aunt seems dejected. When she gets home at night after work she finds Dolores and Lewis in the kitchen. There is a smell of orange zest. Both of them have already had dinner. Maialen is asleep in her room. Lewis tells her that she has a slight fever, and he shows her a picture she drew. When she sees the house with the mountains in the background, she remembers how her mother used to iron the clothes with a little girl by her side drawing little mountains. She can almost hear the *thrum-thrum* sound of the iron and smell the clean clothes, and the headache that she brought from the office starts to evaporate like steam. 'It's for you,' says Lewis. And so it is. Under the drawing of the little house, it says MUM, in capital letters. MUM. Because Mum is a word that should be written in capitals.

She tries to guess what was going through Maialen's mind when she wrote the word *Mum*. What mother is that? The one who shows up at home from time to time? The one that is often not home when she goes to bed? When she was a child, mother and home were the same thing. The house was her mother's realm, the place to seek her mother's protection. But now Maialen cannot identify her home with her mother. With the question of what she identifies it with still unanswered, Lewis tells her he's going to bed, he woke up early this morning and he's tired. He gives her a kiss, and Nerea thinks that if her aunt weren't in the kitchen she could ask her husband for another kiss to conceal the emptiness she feels inside.

She looks at her aunt and realises how gaunt she is. Ever since the story of her mother's past came to light, she can't hold her head up. Nerea suspects that she feels guilty, as if she hadn't offered enough help when her sister needed her. And she realises that, like her aunt, she too bears the weight of guilt on her shoulders. For all the things she didn't say to her mother all her life, but first and foremost because she didn't tell anyone about her mother's condition. The two women each carry a stone, and that stone forces them to get up before anyone else in the morning to get to the hospital as fast as possible, and that stone makes them want to cry when they see Luisa among the white sheets, lost in her own smile.

Nerea looks at her aunt and sees no sign of Tinker Bell from the story. These are different eyes. Dolores makes linden flower tea, saying that she couldn't sleep last night. It seems strange to Nerea to hear her aunt complaining. The original colour of the wardrobe is peeking through. Her aunt's true colours are starting to show.

'You keep going over and over what Mum said to you, don't you?' asks Nerea.

'Yes, I can't get it out of my mind.'

'It's okay, Aunt Dolores, little by little you'll forget.'

'No. I won't be able to forget. Luisa's words have woken so many memories... Now, seeing everything from a distance, I can see more clearly than ever how much your mother suffered at that time, and how little I helped her.'

'But, Aunt Dolores, you can't do anything about it now. You can't change the past,' says Nerea.

'Not the past, Nerea, but you can change the present. And what is past for us has become the present in your mother's mind. Do you realise what that means? It means we could have a second chance.'

'A second chance? To do what?'

'I know you're going to say it's crazy and I must have lost my mind, but I've spent the whole day thinking about it. I've gone over it and over it and it's possible, Nerea, it's possible, but only if you help me. I want to give your mother the help I didn't give her then.'

'But how?'

'It's very simple. By granting her wish... By taking her to the lighthouse.'

'But... now?'

'Why not? It's never too late.'

'Are you serious, Aunt Dolores?'

'I've never been so serious in my life, Nerea, that much I promise you.'

She can almost hear Bittori's voice saying *now we've seen it all!* She can't believe what she's hearing. Her aunt's eyes are wild. Suddenly she thinks Dolores has actually gone crazy, and she doesn't know whether to laugh or cry. Better to do neither, because once she starts laughing or crying, there will be no stopping.

Take her mother to the lighthouse. That's all she needs right now, all that was missing from the to-do list in her appointment book: *take Luisa Izagirre to the lighthouse*. Her aunt really has gone crazy, she thinks.

'She needs to make peace with the sea. It will release her, Nerea. And me too.'

'But it's impossible, Aunt Dolores. We can't take Mum out of the hospital the way she is. Don't you remember what the doctor said? We can't move her from one place to another.'

Dolores goes to the bathroom. She leaves Nerea alone in the kitchen, her words still echoing. Nerea stares at the cup on the table. She hears Lewis coughing in the bedroom. She realises that he's calling for her. She leaves the cup with the dirty dishes and goes to the bedroom with her hands on her hips. Her period is making her kidneys ache.

23

She would like to tell him. 'Do you know what our aunt said, brother? You won't believe it, brother.' But no words come out of her. Because explaining to her brother what her aunt has proposed would mean bringing her mother's hidden history to light. And how would she tell her brother all that? Would he understand anything of it? Or would he put his head in his hands and say 'but what are you two up to?' like Bittori used to say to Aunt Dolores and her mother? 'Leave Mum in peace,' he would say. That's what he would say, thinks Nerea. She is meeting Xabier for lunch.

'We have to make a decision, Nere. We need to decide where to take Mum when she gets out of the hospital. We can't take her back to her house. If she isn't with someone... We'll have to find a place for her somewhere... I don't know, I think we should talk to Aunt Dolores too.'

Her brother's words hurt. It's the first time they have talked openly about the severity of their mother's situation. It hurts her to imagine their mother watching them, the mere thought that she might hear her son and daughter debating where to take her makes Nerea sad. The little girl who drew mountains and farmhouses and the boy who flung toy cowboys to their death are debating what to do with their mother. Where to take their mother. As if their mother were a suitcase. As if she were their aunt's old leather suitcase.

'Yesterday she was saying she wants to go to the lighthouse and I don't know what else.' Xabier tells her what happened at the hospital the previous day, and adds that their aunt looks very upset, beside herself.

'It's hard to believe, eh, brother? How the mind can just *snap*.'

And when she says *snap*, Nerea moves her wrist with the same motion one uses to open a door with a key.

'Yes. And from one day to the next, what's more. Huh, I can understand it when an old person loses her mind bit by bit. That I can understand. But the way it happened to Mum... Losing her mind overnight, without any warning...'

'Don't say that, brother.' Nerea feels like saying don't say that Mum has lost her mind, but her tongue is silent because of what else he said. Warning. A warning that other people didn't see, but she did, and she remembers the day she found her mother making croquettes. Warning. Signs she didn't want to see. She was too busy at work to see anything. Focused on her own things. And now, hearing her brother's words, she remembers some other things too. Things the doctor said. *If we had known earlier...*

She says goodbye to her brother and watches as he walks away. She wonders if he still makes toy cowboys commit suicide when he plays with his son. Has he taught him that game, or would his son rather play Nintendo or PlayStation? Yes, definitely. And he would definitely say to him 'what we played were real games, not like these.' Or not. Maybe he too plays Nintendo.

Like Xabier, Dolores also asks her what will happen when

her mother gets out of the hospital. After spending the whole afternoon at the editorial office, Nerea goes to the hospital to pick her up, and she brings up the topic in the car on the way home.

'In the end I see her in a nursing home,' says Aunt Dolores quickly, almost without leaving spaces between her words. She is looking at the road and perhaps she has gotten used to Nerea's style of driving. She doesn't say a word about her speed.

'Why do you say that, Aunt Dolores?'

'Because it's so. Who will take care of your mother? You? You can't, Nerea. You don't even have time to take care of your daughter...'

A thorn pierces Nerea's breast. It pains her that her aunt would say that.

'Who will take care of her? Tell me. I'd love to but I have to go back to Germany. I have people there I have to take care of too.'

She knows her aunt's tone of voice all too well. Tinker Bell has gone sour. Tinker Bell is tired. She doesn't fly any more, and she doesn't leave sparkles in her wake. Tinker Bell has fallen to earth. She has come down to earth.

'Nerea. Listen, please. In a nursing home or at home or wherever she ends up, your mother's life from now on will take place within four walls. Like in jail. Let's grant her last wish. We can do it, Nerea. Let's take her to the lighthouse and see how the north wind blows in her face, how the wind blows through her hair.'

Nerea looks at her out of the corner of her eye and realises that her aunt's eyes are full of tears. Her chin is trembling. She should give her a tissue or put her arm around her. But she can't take her hands off the steering wheel. They've entered an area where she has to drive carefully. Her aunt presses on.

'For once let's let her do what she wants to do. That's what she wants. Who are we to deny Luisa her dream?'

They get home and eat dinner quickly. Lewis was waiting for them with dinner ready. After dinner, Dolores goes to her room without eating dessert. She barely spoke during the meal. Nerea puts Maialen to bed without reading her a chapter of *Alice in Wonderland*, even though her daughter begged her a thousand times. Today she doesn't feel like telling about how Alice fell down the rabbit hole. It makes her head spin just to think about it.

Lewis asks her what's wrong with Dolores as the two of them brush their teeth together at the sink. Nerea shrugs her shoulders, as if she doesn't know. Then her husband asks her what's wrong. 'Everything, Lewis, everything,' she says with her mouth full of foam. And suddenly she doubts whether she said that correctly in English. Even though she speaks it every day, she will never speak English like Lewis.

As they're going to bed, Lewis suddenly remembers that he has a message for her. Maite called. She had called Nerea's phone but it was turned off. Nerea remembers that she ran out of battery and told Maite to call her at home if she had something to tell her that she thought was important. An image comes to her mind: Karlos.

Maite's phone call reminds her of the days just after Karlos disappeared. Then too Maite called her at home. There were no mobiles in those days. Maite called her at her parents' house to tell her that another two young men had disappeared with Karlos. And with that, Nerea understood everything. No further explanation was necessary. And even if further explanation had been necessary, she wouldn't have found anyone willing to give it.

She said nothing to her parents, but they soon found out.

By the time the police came to their house, they knew that Karlos had disappeared. They asked her a thousand questions, but she at least didn't have to go to the station. She wasn't subjected to the treatment that some of Karlos' other friends had to put up with. Simply remembering what they told her when they came out of the station gives her goosebumps all over her body.

She falls asleep thinking of Karlos and he visits her in her dreams. She sees him at the door to her house, with a long beard, looking like a beggar. She goes to the door with Maialen, where her daughter looks the bearded stranger up and down and asks, 'What does he want, Mum?'

And she has no answer.

24

As with songs when you hear a golden oldie, it is enough for Nerea to see the photos that were hidden to remember Karlos' smell and hear his strong voice. She decided to open today the sealed envelope that she had kept for so many years among the photographs, and there she finds some ten photos, all of them taken with Karlos. Sealed with a kiss before she went to Oxford, the envelope had not been opened until today. From the time she got out of bed, she was thinking about opening the envelope. Ever since she saw Karlos in her dreams. As if she would be able to find in the old pictures the answer to the question Maialen asked in her dream. She puts the envelope in her purse to open it at work. She gets to the office, spreads open a couple newspapers on her desk, and puts the pictures in among the pages without paying attention to the hustle and bustle that gradually increases around her.

She remembers the smell of smoke and grass on the clothes she was wearing that unforgettable time they went camping at Urkiola. In the photo she is sitting outside the tent, smiling at Karlos, who is on the other side of the camera, and hugging a big black dog with her right arm. It's Blackie, Karlos' dog. The only one who asked after his master after Karlos disappeared. Blackie. After he was found on the street, he went over to Nerea and started barking, as if he were asking 'where is Karlos?' But he had no answer from the girl with the bowed head, and he had to head back home because Karlos' uncle was pulling on his leash. Nerea heard the barking even from far away, and the dog left not only his barks but also his question in her mind. Where is Karlos? Where is he?

She remembers their heavy breathing in that Canadian tent. That was where she felt for the first time the heat of a man's body against her belly. She remembers walks with Blackie in the Urkiola forest, and the smell of moss. As she sits in her chair at the office, she closes her eyes and breathes in deeply, as if she wanted to capture again the smell of that humidity. How free she was then. Some of the sweetest memories of her life come back to her when she thinks of camping at Urkiola, and she realises that she had almost forgotten that she was there for a week, sleeping in a Canadian tent, cooking her food over a fire, singing to the sound of a guitar that a friend had brought. And she imagines herself at the Urkiola lookout point, looking toward Mount Anboto and laughing out loud at the sight of that huge chunk of rock, arms raised up over her head. And this image inevitably leads her to another, and a series of stills passes quickly through her mind. In one she is at Urkiola shrieking joyfully into the air, and in another, her mother gazes at the great sea before her and breathes deeply. She feels a tremor deep inside. Her mother at the lighthouse, herself at Urkiola. There is no better image in her mind to represent freedom.

She closes the envelope when she sees that Fidel has come into the editorial office. She puts it away in her purse and raises her hand to her computer mouse. She opens her email programme and sees a message from Maite among all the others. Sent the day before. She's been trying to call, she says, but can't reach her. She wants to warn her. It's nothing really, just that Iñaki had told Karlos where she lives, but not to worry, if she doesn't want to see him, Karlos won't show up on her doorstep.

'Shit,' she says out loud. But no one in the office looks at her. It doesn't matter if she says anything there or not, no one ever looks.

She imagines Karlos in front of her house as he appeared to her in her dream, and she is afraid, but she doesn't know why. She's not afraid of Karlos. How could she be? But the past falling on her like rain frightens her. Because when it's raining, sometimes a few cursed drops fall down her neck and make her whole body shiver. And she doesn't want to shiver. She can't see Karlos, not now at least. She has enough on her plate with her mother.

The stink of Fidel's aftershave reaches her nose. He passes by and drops an announcement for a press conference on her desk. It's within an hour, at noon. She'll take the bus. It's impossible to park in the city centre at noon.

She looks out of the window on the bus and sees heads bobbing up and down in the crowds on the pavements. Any one of those heads could be Karlos, she thinks, and she puts her hand up beside her ear to hide her face. She bites her lower lip, confused and upset.

Then she remembers what her aunt said, that her mother's life from now on will take place within four walls, as if she were in jail, and that they have a chance to free her mother. To make her feel free. Free, like she herself felt at the Urkiola campsite. She hears Blackie barking. The dog is moving away from her in the forest. No one is pulling on his leash the way Karlos' uncle will later.

She closes her eyes and imagines the lighthouse her mother has mentioned so many times. The land is rocky around it. There is a woman on top of a large rock. She has her hands up on either side of her mouth and she is shouting joyfully. That woman is not Luisa Izagirre, nor is it Dolores Izagirre. It's Nerea. Nerea Etxebarria is the person shouting. She breathes in, deeply, strongly, and feels the suffocation of recent days ease, even if only for a few seconds. And when she sees herself facing into the north wind, she forgets everything about the hospital and her fear of seeing Karlos. Everything flies out of her head. Then she feels like shouting, shouting as she looks at the sea, but suddenly realises she is on a bus and has to get off at the next stop.

She can't concentrate at the press conference. Thank goodness she brought her tape recorder. Looking at the speakers, she imagines a car on a narrow road full of curves, the road to the sea. Laughter comes from the car, women's laughter, and as the car moves on, it leaves a shining wake on the road, as if golden dust were pouring from the exhaust pipe.

25

Christmas lights in the hospital. A man in blue overalls is up a ladder hanging lights. He is yelling at his workmate on the ground, saying he installed them wrong or something. Nerea has always loved Christmas because it was the time when her aunt would come home, but this year she suspects she'll feel like puking as soon as she hears the first Christmas carol.

When she goes into the hospital room, she runs into her aunt, who was just leaving to get a breath of fresh air.

'You're early,' says Dolores.

'Yes, I finished early today.'

It's always the same. Her profession makes her late to everything. Late home, late to dinner with friends, late to the hospital... And everyone around her is used to it by now. It's normal for her to be arriving for coffee after the meal, or when Maialen is already asleep. And when she finishes early – and there is no way of knowing in advance when she'll finish – it seems that no one is expecting her and they all look amazed, like her aunt does now. 'Oh, you're here,' say her friends, but they have to set another place at the table. 'Oh, you're here,' says Lewis, but she catches them right in the middle of Maialen's story and spoils the moment.

Her aunt is going out. It's too hot in the room. Nerea has started sweating and has to take her coat off right away. Her mother is aware and looking at the television, which is on, nodding her head yes to everything the presenter says. She seems to be more awake than ever.

'Hi, Mum,' says Nerea, and takes her hand.

Her mother looks away from the television and looks at her for a moment. She has improved in the last week. She smiles at Nerea and raises a finger to point at the television. To say that what's on is very interesting or something like that. She looks like a child. She looks like she has the freedom of a child.

From the other side of the room, Pili says that the show is very entertaining. It must be, thinks Nerea, since the three women watching it can't take their eyes off the screen. Pilar is also watching the television, she's not looking out the window today. And as always, she is silent.

When the show is over, Pili looks like she's about to start clapping, but she doesn't. She sighs instead and says 'Anyway,' undoubtedly thinking that she will never earn the amount of money the contestants have won.

Dolores' purse is on the little table by the side of her mother's bed, open, and Nerea sees part of an old photograph. She picks it up, perhaps thinking that it must be a secret photo she has never seen, perhaps she'll find out what Herman looked like. But no such luck. Her father and mother hold hands in the photograph, with the sea in the background. Their backs are to the sea. Behind them are a few rocks and the sea. Her mother is smiling and the sea breeze from behind her is blowing her hair forward. She is trying to pat her hair back into place with her hand, with a shy gesture. And her father is looking at her mother, also smiling, as if admiring her beauty. He looks like he's telling her mother how beautiful she is, just like Lewis told Nerea in the pub in Oxford. Her mother has her back to the sea. And now she has made a plea to them, Nerea thinks, to see the sea in person. Nerea asks, almost without meaning to.

'Do you really want to go to the lighthouse, Mum?' she asks, still holding her hand.

But her mother just keeps smiling, as if she had heard nothing. Nerea doesn't realise her aunt has come back into the room, and she asks her mother the same question again:

'Do you want to go to the lighthouse, Mum?'

When she hears this question, Dolores' eyes nearly pop out of her head. She stares at Nerea. Her eyes are wide. She could burst at any moment. Then she takes Nerea by the arm and asks her to step outside. She almost drags Nerea into the hall.

'Why did you ask her that?'

Nerea makes an attempt to free her arm, but her aunt holds on tight.

'Are you willing, Nerea?'

Nerea walks toward the elevators, trying to escape from her aunt, but Dolores comes huffing up behind her.

'Aunt Dolores, I still think the same thing. It's crazy. It's very far away and you know what the doctor told us, we can't take her out of here. And besides, do you think Mum is even going to notice?'

'I'm sure she will. She won't have forgotten the smell of the salt. She must have it stashed away in some hidden place in her mind. And she'll remember it when she smells it again. I'm sure she'll remember.'

Nerea imagines her mother looking at a raging sea, hair dancing, hands on either side of her mouth, shouting. Shouting with all her strength. And she is envious. She too would like to shout. Shout, to rid herself of all her fears and shoo away all her ghosts.

'Aunt Dolores, don't you understand...?'

Her aunt doesn't speak to her any more. Even when they leave the hospital and get in the car, she doesn't speak until they arrive at the garage at home. Right in front of the garage, Nerea slams on the brakes. Thank goodness her aunt has her seatbelt on. She almost hits her head on the front windshield.

'What are you doing?' yells Dolores.

Nerea saw a man with a beard on the pavement and was startled. That's why she hit the brakes.

'Nothing, it's nothing... I was just startled, that's all.'

Her aunt asks her if she saw a ghost, her face is so white. And it seems to Nerea that she did indeed see a ghost. The bearded man who passed in front of the car looks at her like she's crazy and then goes into the house next door. When she realises it was just a neighbor putting out the trash, Nerea takes a breath.

'I keep telling you, you drive too fast.'

'No, Aunt Dolores, I know how to drive.'

'You're just like your father, aren't you? You know how to drive, you know how to drive...' Dolores keeps muttering until Nerea gets the car parked.

She has had to do more manoeuvres than ever. It was very difficult to get the car into the narrow space by the wall.

26

She gets into bed and seeks the heat of Lewis' body. Lewis is sitting up in bed with a pillow behind his back. He has some pages and a red pen in his hands. He says he has to finish some corrections. And so he does. He makes a little line here, another one there; he circles a word and sends it from one end of the sentence to the other; he crosses something out here, draws an arrow there. And he reads the text that he's read a thousand times for the thousand and first time. He spends his whole day like this, nose stuck in words, and sometimes it seems to Nerea that he is taking on the colour of the pages. His face seems whiter and whiter.

She snuggles up to his waist, and he keeps on working. With his right hand he pushes his glasses up since they were falling off the end of his nose, and then scratches his head with the end of the pen.

Both of them spend all their energy on the things that need to be done. They have nothing but leftovers for the plate of their relationship, Nerea thinks. When they finish all their work and their chores, if they have a little bit of strength left, they offer it to their spouse, but it's always leftover time, it's always leftover energy, it's always leftover smiles. Nothing but leftovers. Someone else eats the centre. By the time they're together, they have been emptied and they have nothing but crumbs to offer each other.

She would like to talk more with Lewis. Sit down to talk. Not talk while doing something else, but sit down to talk. She would like to tell Lewis the story of her mother's past, for example. So many things have happened to her since her mother went into the hospital. She has learned so many things. She has learned about a hidden side of her mother, and of her aunt too. 'Life is strange, Lewis,' she would like to say to him with a sigh. She would like to stop time for a moment. Stop inside a photograph and live in that moment. She would tell him that when her mother was young, she had a boyfriend named Herman. But how in the end the dream Herman had built had been left unfulfilled. And she would ask him what happens to dreams like that. Where do they end up? Are they lost forever or do they stay in hiding and one day, when it's least expected, rise to the surface?

She would like to sit down at a table and talk. And explain how her aunt can no longer bear the weight of guilt. That she thinks she didn't offer enough help to Nerea's mother and now she wants to make things right by taking her mother to the sea. 'Life is strange, Lewis,' she would like to tell him. 'That's life,' he would answer. And she would also tell him about Karlos, whom she has never even mentioned to him, and tell about his life. She has never told him about Karlos. She has never told him that she is always worried about Karlos, that she always has a ghost in her mind and now that ghost has appeared. She would like to tell him, but she doesn't dare. Nor does she dare to tell him her mother's hidden story.

Nerea says they have to think about where to take her mother when she gets out of the hospital. She has spoken to her brother about it but they haven't decided anything yet. Lewis nods, but keeps working. Underlining words with his red pen, moving words.

And then she tells him that Dolores has suggested taking her mother to the sea. Yes, to the sea. Her aunt says that her mother would love it, that even when she came to the city to live, she still thirsted for the sea. She needed its wide open space. Ever since she married and moved to the city, she has missed it; she suffocates in the city. It would do her good to see the sea a little bit now. She says it all and waits for Lewis' answer.

'But would your mother be aware of anything? Is she aware of anything?' he asks in English, pushing his glasses up again.

'She would be aware of it. The smell of the salt, the sound of the waves on the rocks, the north wind in her face... She would be aware of it. How could she not be?'

They fall silent. Lewis tosses his papers to the floor, takes off his glasses, and lies down. Nerea gives him a kiss. Then she turns out the light on the night table. Lewis' breath gets deeper and deeper. It makes her think of the sound of waves rising and falling.

27

Dolores sees Luisa hiding in a corner of the kitchen.

'Herman is outside, asking for you,' Dolores tells her, frightened by Luisa's white face.

Luisa puts a finger to her lips to tell her to be quiet. She doesn't want to see Herman. She says to say she's running errands. That's what Dolores does, and Luisa waits until Herman has left the restaurant to come out of the kitchen, still shaking.

'Where have you been?' When Bittori sees them, she puts the flower vase from the bar in Luisa's hands and orders her to take them to the young man at the table by the window.

'Will you look up?' orders Bittori. 'And smile at the boy or something.'

Hands still shaking, Luisa grasps the flower vase, but as she goes to place it on the table, it slips and spills all over the young man. He is wet and the flowers are all over his table.

She begs him to forgive her, to please forgive her. Then Luisa learns the name of the young man who has been coming to the restaurant every week for lunch. His name is Paulo, he tells her, while she tries to dry his trousers with a towel from the kitchen.

28

Something unusual happens today with Pili. When Nerea arrives at the hospital, she finds her pacing the hallway, alone. It seems strange. Pili runs to her when she sees her. Wide-eyed and worried, she says that they have taken her mother, Pilar, for some tests and they wouldn't let her go along. Nerea tells her to calm down, and they sit down in the waiting room by the elevators. She holds Pili's hand, she seems so tense, and tells her again to calm down. It occurs to Nerea that this woman wouldn't ever leave her mother alone, and with that thought the conversation she had with Xabier inevitably comes to mind. The mere thought that they were debating what to do with their mother when she gets out of the hospital disturbs her, especially seeing how worried Pili is about her mother. Without letting go of Pili's hands, she tries to calm her down and then they go into the room together. There Pili tells her that when they get out of the hospital, she wants to take her mother to the town where she was born, in Galicia. She believes it will do her good to return. One way or another, her mother is always thinking about going back. Nerea notices something while Pili is telling her all this. Today, for the first time since they met, she is speaking without extra words.

There are nothing but golden words in the prospector's sieve. And those golden words help Nerea to make a decision.

She thought it was crazy to take her mother out of the hospital, put her in a car, and drive her nearly a hundred kilometres, only to sit her down to look at the sea. It really is crazy, especially since the doctor told them that taking their mother out of the hospital will do her no good. But now Nerea is willing to do this crazy thing.

She runs out of the hospital at noon and instead of heading for the office, heads for home. She needs to find her aunt and tell her that she is willing to do this crazy thing and, as always when someone realises that they are about to do something crazy, she feels a unique reaction in her body: her feet move faster, as if her body had no weight. And, as always when someone realises that they are about to do something crazy, she remembers that most of her body is water, and she can feel water currents in her body going up and down, from one side to the other. She feels waves beating against her heart and the foam that rises must come out of her mouth, transformed into words. And, suddenly, everything before her seems rounded and she sees no corners. All the corners are now rounded. Like someone who is about to do something crazy, she sees herself atop a tall summit. Ready to jump. And she feels no fear, because there is water below, and after all, she also is water.

When she gets home, she finds her aunt asleep in front of the television. It is noon. She is rarely home at noon, and the light coming in the living room windows seems strange to her. It looks like weekend light. Since Lewis has a lunch meeting with his editor, he is not here. Dolores is alone, crashed out on the sofa. There is a cup of chamomile tea on the table, full to the brim and cold. She fell asleep before she could take a single sip. It's not surprising, since she barely sleeps at night. She is not expecting Nerea home until the evening. Nerea doesn't want to startle her. If she wakes up and sees her there, she'll start asking questions. What happened, did something serious happen, why is she not at work? And she will try to explain that instead of taking her to work from the hospital, the car brought her home, as if impelled by some mysterious force.

Nerea has hardly ever seen her aunt this still. Her hands are crossed over her belly. She looks like Nerea's mother. Her aunt looks like her mother when she's asleep in her hospital room. Her hands go up and down as her belly rises and falls with her breath. How much work those hands have done, thinks Nerea, how many suitcases they've picked up, how many letters they've written. It can't have been at all easy to be so far from home all those years she has lived in Germany. She left with Sebastian to try to find in Germany what she couldn't find at home. And what was meant to be a round-trip journey became a one-way trip instead. Like a seed sown in fertile ground, their daughter grew there, and they ended up tied to a land that was not theirs, like a ship that has dropped anchor. Like most people who leave their homeland, her aunt must feel a void, she thinks, like the one Pili's mother must feel.

One could hardly believe that the woman before her could fly, seeing her sleeping on the sofa as she is, but seeing the sparkle in her eyes is enough to make one believe it. Dolores is capable of flying and also of filling anything with golden dust.

She wakes up suddenly and is startled, as Nerea thought she would be.

'What are you doing here? What's happened?' she asks. She gets up immediately and stands in front of Nerea.

'Sit down, Aunt Dolores,' says Nerea.

'But how did you come to be here? Aren't you supposed to be at work?' she asks, looking at the watch on her wrist. When she first woke up she didn't know if she was in Frankfurt or somewhere else.

'We have to talk, Aunt Dolores.'

And she sits down again. Nerea's first words are awkward, slow. As if she didn't know where to start. And she really doesn't know where to start. But once she starts, one word follows another and they all slide together, like fish in a net slide one after another when the net is tipped out onto the ground. Nerea thanks her aunt for everything she has done since she came. And then she talks about her mother. The words slide one after another, like the dead fish. Her throat is on fire. She hears her heartbeat in her ears. And it seems that nothing will stop her flow of words.

'Aunt Dolores, I've realised that we can't deny her this.'

She finishes with this sentence. Her aunt smiles and takes her hand. She takes Nerea's hand in her hands that have carried a thousand suitcases and written a thousand letters. And she doesn't speak. It would be hard for her to express in words what the sparkle in her eyes expresses. Nerea sees the gratitude in those eyes.

'If Mum were in her right mind, she'd say we're crazy, Aunt Dolores,' says Nerea.

'Why?' she asks in a shaky voice.

'Because we're about to do a crazy thing.'

Dolores leaps up from the sofa. She looks at Nerea, who nods her head. They hug each other, laughing and crying at the same time. They notice the currents rising and falling in their bodies. They are the currents felt by those who are about to do something crazy.

29

She leaves the editorial office full of joy, with a huge smile she has not worn in a long time. She looks ten years younger in the mirror on the elevator. She has asked for a few days off, citing personal issues. As she leaves, Xabier calls. 'We have to talk.' 'Now?' 'Now,' he says. She feels the water speeding through her veins. They have met at a café in the city centre close to Xabier's office. He is wearing a blue tie and says he has only a little time. He asks what's going on, is their mother okay. Yes, she's okay, says Nerea, but she has something to tell him. It's urgent.

'I know you're going to say we're crazy, brother,' she says once they sit down at a table in the café. 'It's too long a story to explain it all, but in short, we want to take Mum to the sea. Take her out of the hospital and take her to the seashore.'

'What is this, one of Aunt Dolores' crazy stories?' he answers, raising his eyebrows.

'It's not about Aunt Dolores or her stories. It's about Mum.'

He frowns.

'I don't understand a thing, Nere. Don't you remember what the doctor said? It's not advisable to take Mum out of the hospital.'

Xabier raises his voice. With the last sentence, he hits the café table with his hand and sets the cups to dancing.

'You know Mum keeps saying she wants to go to the lighthouse. Aunt Dolores told me that might help her...'

'But don't you two realise that Mum doesn't know what she's saying?'

Again her brother's words hurt her, as they did before when he told her they had to think about what to do with their mother. They fall silent. Xabier sighs and brings his hands to his face.

'Look, Nere, I can't deal with these things. I'm swamped at work, I can't stop worrying about how we're going to manage with Mum when she gets out of the hospital, and now here you are wanting to take her on a wild goose chase. Have you two gone crazy or what? Do you seriously think you know better than the doctors? It would do her good... How do you know?'

'She's aware of more than we think.'

Again Xabier covers his eyes with his hands. He feels bad about saying that their mother isn't aware of anything. He doesn't know what else to say.

The waitress comes over to take their cups. A teaspoon falls from the table to the floor. Xabier picks it up and gives it to her.

'A suicide spoon...' says Nerea, smiling. 'Do you remember how you made the toy cowboys commit suicide by throwing them off the bed?'

Even though his eyes are still frowning, Xabier's mouth laughs.

'And how Mum used to scold me from the kitchen?' he remembers. And his face relaxes.

Nerea's brother looks out the café window thoughtfully. People are running under the awning to escape the rain.

'Is it really all that important?' he asks his sister.

'Yes.'

'Do you know what you're getting yourselves into?'

'Yes.'

'I don't know, Nere, I just don't know...'

The currents of water move here and there inside Nerea. She smiles at her brother again, waiting for his answer. Xabier takes a deep breath, puffs out his cheeks, and exhales.

'But...' he leaves the sentence unfinished, and then laughs. 'You two are a bit crazy, aren't you?'

'Maybe a little bit, brother, just a bit,' Nerea answers, and both of them smile. She would like to explain to Xabier how someone who is about to do something crazy feels, but her brother says he is in a hurry and gets up from the table.

'I don't understand it, but if you two think it's that important...' he says to his sister as he leaves the café. 'And don't forget your umbrella.'

As they say goodbye, she promises him that they'll talk. And her brother's gaze reminds her of the little boy who made his toy cowboys kill themselves a long time ago.

On her way to the car, she calls Maite. She has to tell her that they've decided to take her mother to the sea.

'Maite?'

'Nere...'

Nerea notices that Maite's voice sounds strange, as if something were out of place.

'Is everything okay? Can you talk?' she asks.

Yes, answers Maite, she can talk, she is with Iñaki and some friends... But Nerea notices that she's leaving her sentences unfinished. She tells Maite that they're going to take her mother to the lighthouse. No, they haven't released her yet, it's just for one day. Maite answers in monosyllables.

125

Oh, yes? Good. Yes, yes… But suddenly she interrupts Nerea in the middle of a sentence.

'He's here, Nere. He's with us right now.'

Nerea doesn't need to ask who she's talking about. She knows because of the way Maite said it. It's Karlos. He's with Maite and Iñaki. Her heart starts to pound, and since she doesn't hear Maite's voice, she thinks maybe Maite will hand him the telephone, and she starts thinking about what to say, what to ask, what words to use… But no one is listening on the other end of the line. She hears breathing and that's all. Maite's breathing. Or is it Karlos'? Her heart is in her throat. A thousand photos pass through her mind, a thousand smells, a thousand possible questions.

'Are you there, Nere?'

It's Maite's voice. Nerea forces herself to speak.

'Where are you?'

'In a bar, in Aritz. I'm outside. He's inside with Iñaki.'

'How is he?'

'Fine. Different, but fine. He's watching me from inside, Nere. I think he knows it's you.'

Nerea feels Karlos' gaze. His gaze comes through the phone and goes straight into her breast.

'Do you want to talk to him?'

No words come out. She wants to say no, but she also wants to say yes. She wants to hear his voice but at the same time she doesn't want to hear him. She is afraid that once she hears his voice, her outer layer will fall away and her inner layer will show, the one she has tried to hide all these years. Her knees are trembling and she has to sit down on a bench on the street, even though it's wet from the rain.

'No, Maite. Please tell him I want to talk with him. But not on the phone. I want to see him.'

'Really?'

'Really, Maite. I want to see him. Is he alone?'

'No. Well, right now he is, but he told us he has a wife and son. They're in France, waiting for him to make a decision. He didn't want to bring them until his situation is completely clear. I don't know if he'll be able to live in peace here. He told us they have to make a decision.'

'Tell him we'll see each other. Soon.'

'I'll tell him, Nere. You know what? He's smiling at me from inside the bar... That much hasn't changed. It's his same old smile.'

When Nerea hangs up the phone, she smells a familiar smell and it seems to her that she sees Karlos' smile. They are in the mountains, throwing sticks as far as they can for Blackie, and Karlos is laughing because Blackie has come back with a bigger stick in his teeth than the one he threw. She takes a deep breath. Yes, the smell is the smell of damp moss in the Urkiola forest. Even though she's in the middle of the city.

She doesn't know how long she's been sitting on the bench. It's wet from the rain. Until the rain starts up again she doesn't move from there. She arrives home with her hair wet. She is carrying her umbrella in her hands, as if she had forgotten she had it; she didn't open it on the way. She finds Lewis fixing dinner. Dolores is not yet back from the hospital. Maialen is in front of the television, eyes glued to the cartoons. Nerea goes over to her but as soon as she starts talking, Maialen tells her to be quiet, she can't hear what Doraemon is saying, and not to touch her since she's all wet. 'Okay, okay,' she says and goes away.

She hugs Lewis around the waist, with the urgency of someone shipwrecked holding onto a life preserver, and rests her face against his back. 'Mmmm,' says Lewis when he tries a spoonful of the soup he's making. Then he has Nerea try it and of course she has to say 'mmmm' too, even though it's soup out of a packet. Her ear is pressed against Lewis' back and she can hear his heart beating. When they first met in that dark Oxford pub, she felt her heart start beating faster. Definitely. Especially when he told her she was very beautiful. Now, knowing Lewis as she does, she's sure that he must have been very nervous saying such a thing to a foreign girl. Even though she's remembering things that happened in Oxford, she can't get Karlos out of her mind. For years he has not been as near to her as he is today. She feels like she has already spoken with him. She thinks the time has come to talk to Lewis about Karlos. She has to open that part of her life to him because she realises that it will be like speaking magic words, and that mentioning Karlos' name to Lewis will make the ghost disappear, the one that's been following her for so many years.

When Dolores returns, they eat dinner and, seeing everyone together around the table, Nerea remembers evenings when she ate dinner with her father, her mother and her brother. She sees her mother serving the soup, and her father trying to catch her around the waist while her mother eludes him. Luisa gets away, laughing as if to say not to do such things in front of the children.

Lewis asks her what she's laughing about, seeing her smiling and lost in her own thoughts. She shakes her head and tells her daughter it's time for bed.

'Will you tell me my story tonight, Mum?' Maialen asks as they go to her room hand in hand.

Instead of *Alice in Wonderland*, she would rather tell her daughter about how one feels when one is about to do something crazy. And then say that she is feeling that way herself right now. But there will be time for that later.

'Tonight yes, Maialen,' she answers. 'Tonight I'll tell you about the conversation Alice had with a cat. It wasn't just any old cat, was it? It could appear and disappear.'

And just like the cat in the tree that disappeared from Alice's view, mother and daughter disappear down the hall.

30

There is no longer an old Telefunken in the living room. A more modern television set took its place long ago. They bought it for their parents a year before their father died. Nerea's mother and father spent that last year almost without leaving the house because of her father's illness.

As soon as she opens the door to her mother's house, she notices a closed-up smell. She has come from time to time since her mother has been in the hospital, to fetch something for her mother and water the plants, but until today she has not smelled that closed-up smell. She goes into the living room and stands staring at the television. Then she remembers that that was where the old Telefunken was, and on top of it, a photograph. Black and white. The one in which her mother's hands are cupping her chin. Now there is nothing on top of the television, and the photo is on a shelf with several others. There is a photo from her parents' wedding day, one from Xabier's birthday, and the one in which her mother is cupping her chin. Moments stolen from life are there. In front of the encyclopedia. Covered with dust.

She looks toward the window and sees the geraniums drooping. She opens the window and touches their leaves.

They look dead, but appearances are deceiving. It's a tough plant. When it has no water, it lies dormant, but once it's been watered, it gains strength again and by the time spring arrives, it is ready to flower. She wants to believe that her mother is like that. That her mother also has the strength of the geranium. That she's not dead, that she'll revive in contact with water, and by springtime will be ready to start flowering, to start speaking like she did before. In the same way that flowers bloom on the geranium, words will start flowing from her mouth.

She goes into her mother's room, looking for appropriate clothing for their planned excursion to the lighthouse. Silence reigns all over the house, but as she steps into her mother's room, she thinks she hears the sound of a song from far away. It is her mother's voice; it lingers here, stuck to the walls of the room. Nerea has to swallow hard before she opens the wardrobe. She starts looking for a heavy coat and when she starts moving all the clothes that are hanging there, she smells camphor and suddenly an image comes to her. A little girl is hidden in her mother's wardrobe and her mother is calling 'Where is Nerea? where is Nerea?' from outside it, even though she knows her daughter is hidden inside. The little girl will leap suddenly from the wardrobe and the mother will look surprised and say 'What a fright you gave me' and 'Where were you?'

She chooses a coat. She puts it on the bed and keeps looking. She looks through a drawer in the wardrobe and takes a silk scarf out of it. She sniffs it before throwing it on top of the coat and smells camphor. She thought she would smell her mother's own smell, or the smell of the perfume she used to wear on Sundays, but so far all she smells is camphor, on everything in the wardrobe.

Before she closes the wardrobe, she picks up a small folder from the drawer where she found the scarf. She opens it and finds handwritten pages. The first explains how to make an apple cake. It's in her mother's handwriting. How much flour, how many eggs, how much sugar are needed to make the pastry. It's on a piece of yellowed graph paper. It's the recipes she wrote out in the days of the Izagirre Restaurant. Sea bream in sauce, tuna in tomato sauce, rice pudding. There are a lot of recipes and some have been splattered with oil. American sauce, green sauce. Even though she's never heard Bittori's voice, Nerea can almost hear her dictating the recipes to her mother. Crème caramel, walnut cream. A drop of oil has made it impossible to read several of the words because the ink has spread and, looking at the trace left by the oil spot, Nerea thinks the circle on the paper could be one of her mother's tears. She sees her mother writing out recipes, doing her punishment. One hundred grams of flour, two tablespoons of sugar. The thorns that pierced her mother's belly as she wrote those recipes have been broken with the passage of time and space and now enter Nerea's belly.

She closes the folder and puts it back in its place. She leaves the room and goes down the hall toward the front door. On her way she glances at the kitchen without going into it, and tries to remember the table that used to be in the middle of the kitchen floor. It's not there anymore. It has been more than ten years since her mother redid the kitchen. She put in a glass-ceramic cooktop. It was there that Nerea found her once, making croquettes, forgetting how to make croquettes. A daughter of the Izagirre Restaurant, of all people! Undoubtedly Bittori had made her write out the recipe for croquettes too.

The other times she has come to the house since her mother has been in the hospital, she has come and gone quickly.

Always in a hurry to be somewhere else. But today she is free to poke around in all the corners of the house. Before she leaves, she goes into her old room. Hers and Xabier's are the rooms that have changed the least. She knows each thing in her room like the back of her hand. The pillows on the bed, the rug, the things on the bulletin board on the wall: concert tickets, an anti-nuclear sticker, a pro-amnesty badge, another that says *Don't step on the grass, smoke it*. They are frozen in time, like the photographs. These too are moments stolen from life. She remembers Karlos, and thinks that seeing Karlos will be like coming into this room. Because Karlos is also a room that's been closed for years.

She leaves the room and stops by the door to look down the hall. She remembers her aunt's words. 'No matter where she ends up, your mother's life from now on will take place within four walls.' She smells the closed-up smell again. Carrying the coat and scarf, she goes out and as she turns the key in the lock from outside, she takes a deep breath. So deep that she thinks she can smell the salt of the sea.

31

If she hadn't made the decision to take her mother to the lighthouse, she would be at the office at this hour, she thinks. Setting her cigarette in the ashtray. Instead, she's at home. She took Maialen to the bus and came back home slowly, with two croissants she bought at the bakery. When she gets back home, she invites Lewis to have breakfast again. Lewis makes tea again, and she puts the coffee on again. Dolores left early for the hospital. As she did with Maialen, she gave Nerea a kiss on the forehead before racing out the door. And at that moment Nerea felt like a little child, and felt relieved.

At some moments the water currents inside her subside and she feels like she's stepping into warm water. That's what she feels at this moment. The two of them sit down to breakfast a second time at the kitchen table and, seeing her husband across from her, the situation looks like a moment she has dreamed about many times. She is sitting at a table with Lewis. They are face to face. Looking at each other. Ready to speak. And the sun comes in the window.

Lewis laughs when his wet croissant falls into his tea and asks her if his croissant just committed suicide. They laugh, and Nerea says not to laugh because in her family there's a history of suicide. Lewis' smile freezes for a moment, but he quickly realises she's joking. Her brother used to make his toy cowboys commit suicide, she explains, by making them jump off the bed. And Lewis says that he can't imagine Xabier making his cowboys kill themselves. Nerea admits that, for someone who didn't know him as a child, it is hard to imagine today's Xabier, with his tie and everything, making his cowboys commit suicide.

'I wish I could go with you tomorrow,' says Lewis.

'Really?'

Lewis wouldn't believe how happy it makes Nerea to hear that.

'Yes. I don't know for sure what meaning it has for you two to go see the sea, but you've changed since you made the decision.'

'Changed? What was I like before, then?'

'Well, you were pretty upset, weren't you? We haven't even had a chance to talk since this thing with your mother started.'

He tried, says Lewis, but it was like talking to a wall. Nerea didn't listen to anything. And he didn't dare to say anything because she looked like she would shatter if he touched her.

She gets up from her chair and tells Lewis to wait. Just wait right there for a minute. She returns with her purse. She takes an envelope out of it. There are some ten photographs in it, the ones taken at the Urkiola campsite.

'Look, do you see this girl here with the dog?'

Lewis looks curiously at the pictures. It's the first time he's seen them.

As if she had cut a ball and chain from her ankle, she feels lighter when she leaves the house. When she gets to the hospital, she finds her aunt in the bathroom of her mother's room, dyeing her mother's hair. Dolores is startled when Nerea enters the bathroom, thinking she must be a nurse. Her mother's eyes are very wide. Her hair is wet. She looks like a little girl who has just come out of the water. Her mother looks like a child who has just come out of the water at the beach and stands there shivering with a towel over her. Like such a child, her gaze is fixed on a single point.

Once they've dried her mother's hair and taken her back to her bed, Nerea, Dolores, and Pili go out of the room and sit in the chairs by the elevators to make plans for the following day. They need to agree on a way to get Nerea's mother out of the hospital.

32

She wakes up before the alarm. She waits between the sheets, unable to get back to sleep because she's waiting for the alarm to go off. It seems to her that Lewis moved around more than ever that night. As if he wanted to claim her part of the bed even before she got up. And even though she had spent the whole evening yawning, she got almost no sleep.

She goes out into the hallway and sees that someone is in the bathroom. She can see the light through the crack in the door. It's her aunt. She has also gotten up earlier than necessary. Undoubtedly, she couldn't sleep.

At breakfast, Dolores confirms this. She was very nervous all night and the wind was blowing hard against the blind. *Clack, clack, clack.* She heard the blind clacking endlessly, she says, and there's no sleeping with that going on. *Clack, clack, clack.*

When Nerea starts pouring the coffee, Lewis gets up. He tells them not to worry, he'll take care of Maialen, but to call him as soon as they get there. Call him, please, and tell him everything that happens.

Maialen appears at the kitchen door barefoot, rubbing her eyes with the sleeve of her pyjamas. She has never woken up this early.

'What is it, Maialen?' asks Nerea.

She runs to her mother and jumps in her lap. Thank goodness Nerea put her coffee cup down on the table. Maialen buries her head in Nerea's chest as if she wanted to hear her mother's heartbeat. She curls up and gathers herself into a knot, like when she was inside her.

'Did we wake you up, sweetheart?' asks Dolores, stroking her cheek.

But Maialen does not answer. She raises her head and looks at her mother. From top to bottom, the way Alice looks at the Cheshire Cat. And like Alice, Maialen has a question.

'Where are you going?'

Nerea wants to say, to work, or grocery shopping, or anything else. But from deep inside her, it comes out.

'To see the sea.'

'I want to go too.'

Nerea smiles and pushes the hair back off Maialen's face.

'You can go too, but another time, okay?'

'No, Mummy, now,' she begs.

'Do you know what we'll do? I'll take a picture of the sea, okay? And then I'll show it to you later.'

She does not agree, but Dolores says she has a little something for her in her room and she forgets about the ocean. She jumps down from Nerea's lap and runs after Dolores to her room.

It's Saturday morning. And when Nerea goes out with her aunt she finds very little movement on the street. A man with a loaf of bread and a newspaper, a young man going to sports practice… She left the car out of the garage last night and goes to bring it around. The sun has come up early today. The air is fine and cool, but after looking at the sky, Dolores says it will be a beautiful day, and they are both happy. The sky is as blue as can be. It looks like it will be one of those sunny winter days. Thank goodness it's not raining, thinks Nerea.

The time has come to put into action the plan she and her aunt and Pili agreed upon the night before. They are at the hospital. They dress Luisa, and Dolores combs the hair that she dyed the day before. With proper clothes on, Luisa looks ten years younger. Nerea had forgotten what her mother looked like without a nightgown. She looks pretty. She hasn't lost her smile. They seat her in a wheelchair. Pilar is staring fixedly at Luisa as if she too would like to get dressed and go out. But as always, she doesn't open her mouth.

Before leaving the room, Nerea goes over to Pilar and Pili. She says she hopes that they can take Pilar home as soon as possible and then she wants to say something more to them, thinking that she will surely never see them again, but nothing comes out of her mouth. Pili can't speak either, strange as it may seem. Nerea hugs Pili and holds Pilar's hand. 'Goodbye,' she says, and that's all. Pilar doesn't answer, she just looks at her, but when Nerea turns and heads for the door, she hears the woman's strong voice behind her.

'Good luck,' she says. As is the case every time this woman speaks, it seems to Nerea that her words must weigh like stones. Good luck.

She turns and smiles at her from across the room. She nods her thanks. She would have liked to say it in words, but her throat is tight, and she realises that no words will come out.

With an ache in her throat, Nerea goes out into the hallway with her aunt and her mother. Slowly they approach the area in front of the lifts, as if they were just going for a little stroll. When they reach the lifts, they hear Pili's voice from the room calling for the nurses like crazy. One goes over to her and, after hearing what Pili says, shrugs her shoulders as if she doesn't know what to say. She looks back and calls another nurse over.

Pili is waving her arms wildly and explaining. Yes, yesterday a nurse told her that her mother had to start a new medication today, but they haven't brought anything... The nurses ask her who told her that, and now it is Pili who shrugs. Eyes on the ceiling, she says she can't remember the name. What was it? What was it again? They call for a third nurse, hoping to figure out what Pili is saying and, taking advantage of the confusion, Nerea and her aunt push her mother into the lift in her wheelchair. Once in the lift, they close their eyes and Nerea smiles to think about Pili's diversion.

When they reach the ground floor, Dolores goes over to the doorkeeper and tells him they're going out to the park, there are only two such sunny days in a year and they have to take advantage of them. The doorkeeper says she's right and tells them to go ahead.

When they reach the parking lot and start helping Nerea's mother into the car, it seems to Nerea as if they're doing something illegal, robbing a bank and making a getaway, each with a stocking over her head. Luisa's eyes are wide. She recognises that something unusual is going on, as if she could hear her sister's and her daughter's heartbeats. She frowns and, seeing her face, it seems to Nerea that everything will go wrong for them. She is worried, remembering what the doctor said. They put Luisa in the passenger seat, Dolores sits in the back, and off they go.

'We're on our way,' she says to her mother, trying to rid herself of the knot in her throat. 'To the lighthouse, Mum, we're going to the sea.'

Nerea's mother turns her head toward her, but Nerea

doesn't know if she's looking at her or at the people she sees through the window at Nerea's side. Yes, she's looking outside. At the people hurrying along the street. She doesn't see her daughter, she's not listening to what she says. Nerea thinks then that what they're doing is foolish, and she remembers Xabier's words. *Have you two gone crazy or what?* He's right. They have gone crazy and she doesn't know what they think they're doing. She can almost hear Bittori's voice, saying they've got bats in the belfry. Scolding them.

She steals a glance at her aunt in the back seat. Dolores doesn't hear Bittori's words. She doesn't realise that they're doing a foolish thing. Luisa is not going to remember anything, and what's more, it's risky to take her so far from the hospital. Dolores is staring at her sister in the front seat and talking to her. They're on their way, she says, get ready to smell the sea salt.

They drive out of the city and after a few kilometres get onto a road full of curves. Until then, Nerea has been able to look across at her mother, but now that the road zig-zags so much, she can't turn her head. As she's watching the road, however, she hears a sentence that nearly stops her cold.

'Another one down!'

It comes after they pass a tight turn. It is a woman's voice, but not her aunt's. For a moment, she feels like she has dunked her head in a pool of the past, as if she has dived into a swimming pool full of water. She sees herself in an old car on the coast road, her father driving. He is driving two women and he's sweating.

No one says anything else. She thinks she dreamed it, but when she feels her aunt's trembling hand on her shoulder, she knows what just happened. It *was* her mother. Her mother called out the sentence her husband used to say to himself a long time ago. *Another one down*! And now she looks as if she hadn't said a word. She's just looking at the road again.

Nerea can't tell whether her aunt is laughing or crying. She can't look because she has to keep watching the road. Suddenly, it seems as if the car is going on its own, as if it knew the way. Then she remembers her dream, and knows that Tinker Bell's fairy dust is pouring out of the car's exhaust pipe. She looks in the rear-view mirror and sees a sparkle, but then she thinks perhaps it was nothing but a reflection of the sun.

33

Seen from the sea, from a small skiff, there are three women next to the lighthouse, looking at the sea. They stand at the edge of the cliff, like seagulls on rocks, and all three are leaning forward so far, it looks like they might jump at any moment. The one in the middle is seated in a wheelchair.

Seen from land there is the wide sea and in the distance, lots of small skiffs are still out on the water. Out of the corner of her eye, Nerea sees her mother at her side. The wind is blowing her mother's hair back, and from her neck a snake zig-zags in the wind as if trying to flee. It is the scarf that they put on her so she wouldn't be cold, the one Nerea took out of the wardrobe and smelled yesterday. After so long in camphor, it has taken on a new life and it looks as if it wants to slither away.

They are still, looking at the sea, until they see a big wave coming toward them. When the wave breaks against a rock, the seagulls leap into the air, calling and crying. Then Nerea feels her mother's hand take hers. A second wave hits the rock, and in addition to her mother's cool hand, Nerea feels the crash of the wave under her feet, and hears the gush of the water. And when the third wave, which is always the strongest, breaks into foam, her mother holds her hand tighter, and she almost hears her mother's voice, even though she doesn't say a word. 'Raise your head, Nerea,' she says, and Nerea remembers her mother's hand cupping her chin. Obeying her mother, she raises her head and, looking past the foam around the rocks, gazes at the horizon, chin up and away from her chest, the same way Bittori Izagirre is looking at the photographer in the picture taken at the restaurant.

She has not looked at the sea like this, straight out at the sea, since she was a child. Since the time when she used to build walls of sand on the beach. Then, kneeling inside her ship of sand, she faced down the waves as they came nearer and nearer, even though she knew that in the end, they would destroy her ship. Nevertheless, she defended her small realm with tooth and claw. With her jaw firmly set. As she does today, thanks to her mother. Her mother lets go of her and returns her hand to her lap, where it rests quietly next to the other. Then she sighs, as one does at the end of a task. Nerea looks at the veins in her mother's hands, highways full of curves, and smiles. It occurs to her that finally her mother's hands have spoken to her, as she once believed they would.

'An exquisite novel by a great new talent.'
M. J. HYLAND

PIGEON
ALYS CONRAN

'...might have been authored by
Faulkner...pitch-perfect.'
OMAR SABBAGH,
NEW WELSH REVIEW

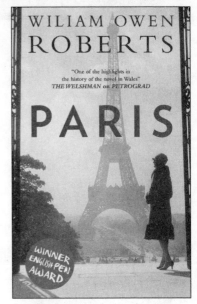

WILIAM OWEN
ROBERTS

"One of the highlights in
the history of the novel in Wales"
THE WELSHMAN on PETROGRAD

PARIS

WINNER
ENGLISH PEN
AWARD

PARTHIAN
A CARNIVAL OF VOICES

THE HOUSE OF THE DEAF MAN
Peter KRIŠTÚFEK

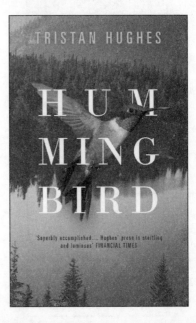

TRISTAN HUGHES

HUM MING BIRD

'Superbly accomplished... Hughes' prose is startling
and luminous' FINANCIAL TIMES

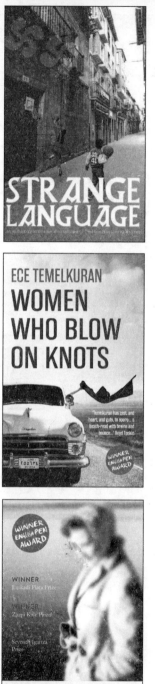

BAD IDEAS\CHEMICALS
LLOYD MARKHAM

STRANGE LANGUAGE

THE EQUESTRIENNE
URŠUĽA KOVALYK

ECE TEMELKURAN
WOMEN WHO BLOW ON KNOTS

A Glass Eye
Miren Agur Meabe

Her Mother's Hands
Karmele Jaio